THE GHOST TIES A DOUBLE KNOT

I0678415

FOURSQUARE BOOKS

THE GHOST TIES A DOUBLE KNOT

THE GHOST TIES A DOUBLE KNOT

A Nell Bane Novel

Nancy Parsons

THE GHOST TIES A DOUBLE KNOT
Nancy Parsons

Published by
The Cheshire Press
A Division of The Cheshire Group, Inc.
PO Box 2090
Andover, MA 01810
www.cheshirepress.com

ISBN: 978-0-9960210-3-6
Library of Congress Control Number: 2014943162

Printed in the United States of America

This is a work of fiction. Any resemblance to individuals or
occupations are purely coincidental. All trademarks used herein are for
identification only and are used without intent to infringe on the
owner's trademarks or other property rights.

Parsons, Nancy
The Ghost Ties A Double Knot

To the memory of
Jack
Writing room companion
and beloved collaborator

Also by Nancy Parsons

More From The Better Mousetrap
with Dick Amsterdam

Bald As A Bean: The Experience of Sudden Hair Loss

Abigail's Unicorn

Ye Canna Join In Oor Games
Memories of a Scottish-American Childhood

Brothers of War: The P.O.W. Experience
with James F. Arsenault

The Dog That Managed Hedge Funds

Two-Thirds of a Ghost
A Nell Bane Novel

The Ghost Works A Puzzle
A Nell Bane Novel

THE GHOST TIES A DOUBLE KNOT

It's a long, long while from May to December
But the days grow short when you reach September
When the autumn weather turns the leaves to flame
One hasn't got time for the waiting game.

Kurt Weill

THE GHOST TIES A DOUBLE KNOT

Chapter 1

"They were great friends of my parents," Robert Hutchins said. "Tice may seem a bit brusque at first but your charm will win the day."

"Tice," repeated Nell. "Unusual name."

"It's Prentice. " Robert said. "And there are very few people left on the earth who can get away with calling him Tice. His wife Arabella is one of course, and for some reason, I seem grandfathered in."

Robert fell silent. Nell waited. She knew there was a story in the wings and while she was eager to hear it, she also knew her old friend. The story would come when Robert was ready to tell it. Nell, watching him, thought of *Il Penseroso*.

"Caroline was diagnosed with an aggressive melanoma," said Robert, picking up the narration. "Bella will tell you her daughter died of cancer, but in fact, Caroline died by her own hand. She decided to beat the cancer to the punch. She didn't want cancer to win so she took matters into her own hands. She raced it and she cheated it of victory."

Robert shook his head.

"I can hardly blame her."

Nell, who didn't yet know these characters Robert was naming, shook her head sympathetically.

"So hard," she murmured. "So unfair."

"Their son George died of a sudden coronary on the thirteenth hole of a Santa Clara golf course," Robert continued. "The irony is his golf partner was a cardiologist with a defibrillator in his car. But the thirteenth was the furthest hole from the parking lot apparently, and by the time they matched up the defibrillator with George, it was too late. There'd been no signs of heart trouble and an autopsy revealed a congenital heart defect. Nobody detected it. Nobody could have predicted it, but bam! For George, it was over. And for Tice and Bella, it was just seven short months after losing Caroline. And so— within the span of a single year—both their children were gone."

Robert fell silent again.

Nell joined his silence, allowing Robert to revisit whatever private grief he carried. As she waited, she took stock of the lovely and familiar room. It reflected the deliberate taste of Robert's partner, designer Jerry Gasso, who complained loudly, frequently and factiously about the hundreds of books that had to be incorporated into the life of the room. But Nell knew Jerry understood that the books were as much a part of Robert's life as his horn-rimmed glasses or his precisely knotted ties.

"Well." Robert pulled himself together. "Caroline and George had one child each. Marriages and careers took both families away from New England. Caroline's marriage was unfortunate and short, and she took her daughter Martha and moved to Florida years ago. George and his wife Barbara were the parents of Michael. George traveled a good deal for business, mostly on the West Coast and sometimes even in

Asia. As a result of distance, Tice and Bella never had the opportunity to be well acquainted with their grandchildren, and though they have several great-grandchildren, they hardly know them at all. So fast-forward to the present..."

He held Nell's gaze.

"Tice and Bella are getting quite old. Tice, in fact, is ninety-one; Bella, I believe is several years younger. But by any standard, the Etons are in advanced old age. And now that they believe themselves about ready to 'go on to greener pastures,' as they put it, they have gotten the notion that they need to prepare their grandchildren—and especially their great-grandchildren—for the legacies they are about to inherit."

Nell waited. She was sure she had a part to play in this drama, but she didn't yet know what it would be. Never mind, she could be patient.

"The Etons have significant wealth," Robert continued.

Nell smiled. She well knew and appreciated Robert's tendency toward understatement.

"Theirs is an old family and their money is old as well. Much of it was inherited. There were Etons living and doing business in Salem back when the Custom House was thriving; they made money hand over fist in those days and just kept at it. Prentice followed his father into finance and added considerably to the pile. Even so, the Etons have always lived very simply. Frugal Yankees."

For some reason this made Robert Hutchins smile.

"Tice and Bella have respected the wealth they've earned, as well as what they've inherited, and they respect the people from whom it came. Tice and Arabella have been good stewards of their wealth. They've established charitable trusts and their philanthropies are well known in Salem and in Boston. They are leading contributors to the Peabody Essex Museum, the Boston Symphony and a number of other worthy non-profits.

Even so, there is a bucketful that will go to their heirs when the second one of them dies—and given their advanced ages, that time can't be too many years away. They wish to prepare their heirs for what is coming."

"Interesting," said Nell drily. "And please tell me Robert, why am I here in your living room listening to this?"

Robert smiled again. "I was coming to that, but perhaps the Etons themselves should tell you. It is, after all, their story to tell."

Chapter 2

North Federal Square, Nell supposed, drew part of its name from the Common it fronted, but the street's name could just have well been coined to describe the houses along its way. Upstanding, Federal houses for the most part, where symmetry was the architectural rule, marched along the Common's north border, and the Etons' house was especially pleasing. Built of good red brick, its white-trimmed windows were ornamented with painted keystones and set off with sharp black shutters. A visitor would climb a set of granite steps and enter between a set of painted Ionic columns. Low iron pickets fenced the property from the sidewalk. Robert had told Nell that the Eton's house was one of the last private residences in the neighborhood; most of these handsome houses had been divided into condos—enviable and pricey ones—and Nell supposed this would be the fate of the Eton house when its owners, as Robert Hutchins had put it, 'went on to greener pastures.' As Nell climbed the granite stairs, she imaged barges floating the slabs down from the Rockport quarries.

"Good afternoon. I'm Nell Bane."

"Why of course you are," said the lovely woman who held the door wide.

Her hair was brilliantly white. Her eyelids drooped slightly at the outer corners, giving a triangular look to her eyes which were sharp and clear and perfectly reflected the color of the periwinkle cardigan she was wearing. A set of pearls and a pair of spectacles on a chain hung about her neck.

"As you probably surmised, I am Arabella Eton. Robert is already here. In the living room with my husband."

Nell stepped into a wide hall that was balanced on each side by living and dining rooms. Mrs. Eton gestured her toward the right. Robert Hutchins rose as the women entered but the man Nell took to be Prentice Eton did not. He was a slight man and would have appeared delicate if it weren't for a vitality of spirit that seemed to vibrate toward her. He turned his wheelchair toward Nell and addressed her.

"Please forgive me, my dear, for failing to rise. I haven't stood for a lady for the past four years and I find myself apologizing for it over and over."

He smiled warmly however and thrust out his hand for Nell to shake.

She smiled in return.

"Mr. Eton, this is a great pleasure to meet you. Robert has told me just a little about your idea—just enough to pique my curiosity. I hope you're prepared to satisfy it."

Prentice Eton laughed and looked over at Robert.

"Just as you said. This young lady will get along very well with Bella and me. Well," he continued, "I think some sherry is in order while we get to know each other. Robert, my boy, will you do the honors?"

And Nell found herself seated on a sofa with Arabella Eton, accepting the small glass of sherry that Robert passed. With an expectant expression, she looked from one Eton to the other.

"Cheers, dears." Prentice Eton raised his glass.

And he began his tale.

"Arabella and I had two children," he said slowly. "Both now deceased. Their deaths are perhaps the greatest sorrow of our lives."

Nell, glancing out of the corner of her eye at his wife, saw her nod very slightly but her tranquility seemed undisturbed and she sat with her chin raised.

"The Etons," Prentice continued, "are not a prolific family. Arabella and I were blessed to have a son and a daughter, but our children married and produced only a single child each. We did not have the opportunity to know these grandchildren well because their parents chose to live in the furthest reaches of the country. Caroline raised her daughter Martha in Florida, while our son George lived in California with his wife Barbara; they lived just north of San Francisco for some years, and then in some of the southern parts—San Diego, Santa Clara and so forth."

He paused. "But I imagine Robert told you some of this."

Nell nodded.

Prentice Eton continued. "George and Barbara had one child—their son Michael. We were to realize that if the Eton name were to be carried on, it would be up to Michael to do it. Both George and Caroline died much too soon."

He looked at his wife. "Do you want to explain, my dear?"

Arabella Eton was perfectly calm as she took up the narration.

"Our daughter was diagnosed with melanoma," she said. "It was that relentless Florida sun. I'm sure of that. I don't think there was the appreciation for sunscreen that we have now, and I'm sure Caroline wasn't careful. She loved the beach. She'd spend hours reading beside the pool."

Arabella shook her head considering this.

"This was not a skin cancer that responded well to treatment or else it was diagnosed too late, but at any rate, the cancer killed her. She died of melanoma," Arabella Eton concluded firmly.

Nell dared a veiled glance at Robert Hutchins who did not meet her eyes. Well, she had been warned of this.

Arabella Eton seemed determined to finish.

"We lost our son George just seven months later—and very suddenly. Very shockingly. He died of a coronary on a golf course. We found out later that he had a congenital abnormality that could have taken him at any time—perhaps while he played a sport at school or perhaps while simply walking on a California beach. Perhaps we should be grateful we had him as long as we did. But tragically, his son Michael was only eight when his dad died. And Barbara—our daughter-in-law—lost no time in remarrying. She married again within the year and that was that. Our grandson had a new father and was removed another few degrees from us. Barbara was not...well, she was not sensitive to family, either to us or to Michael who never really had the chance to know his grandparents."

"So," said Prentice Eton, taking over the narrative responsibility from his wife who, it seemed to Nell, was retiring into her private sorrow. "Within the space of one year we lost our children, but even more was lost. We lost an entire generation. And our grandchildren, and subsequently our great-grandchildren, lost the link that would have connected the generations. The key generational link. The linchpin of family."

Nell ventured a mild question.

"Did you not see your grandchildren after that? After your son and daughter died?"

"We saw them only occasionally. Upon special occasions. We made the trip to California for Michael's high school graduation and again when he married. That's another story—and an interesting one—but for now, somewhat beside the point. And we saw Caroline's daughter Martha a few times as well. We visited in Florida several times but Martha made very little effort to visit New England. She didn't have an especially happy life, I believe. She'd never really known her father and she was still in school when Caroline died, then she rushed into a marriage that was...well, rather marginal."

A woman appeared in the living room door.

"Excuse me, Bella, but you asked not to delay lunch beyond twelve-thirty." She smiled engagingly. "So I'm reminding you."

"Oh! You're quite right, Henny. Thank you."

Arabella Eton stood and the ever-courteous Robert was on his feet in an instant.

"Tice, you can continue your story over lunch," she said. She turned to Nell. "Perhaps you'd like to freshen up? Let me show you the way."

"Robert, my boy," Prentice said, "May I prevail upon you to propel me to the dining room?"

The table in the dining room was laid for four. From a quick inventory of the table setting Nell discerned there would be soup and white wine. The spot at the head table lacked a chair and it was into this spot that Robert rolled Tice's wheelchair and parked it. Robert was asked to pour a little white wine into the glasses while Henny served the soup—a delicate mushroom broth. Nell, savoring it, detected a distant flavor of Madeira.

Prentice Eton offered a few prayerful words for the meal that had been prepared, and Arabella's spoon coasted into the broth as the signal for the meal to begin.

Prentice picked up the thread of his story as the soup was

slowly consumed.

"Caroline's marriage was unfortunate," he began. "Neither Bella nor I approved of Elison Danforth, her husband, but Caroline was over the moon about him. That infatuation lasted a mere five years, but by the time it crashed and burned, she had young Martha whom she elected to raise in Ponte Vedra Beach."

Henny removed the soup plates, then a luncheon plate with a small green salad and a slice of omelet was placed before Nell.

"We went to California when Michael married Crystal."

Remembering this, Prentice shook his head in disbelief. Then he looked down the table and met his wife's eyes. They both laughed. Robert and Nell waited expectantly to hear the reason.

"The Last Hippie," Arabella said. "That's what Crystal, Michael's wife, is called. Apparently her parents—whether they were married or not, we never knew—lived in the mountains of northern California in the days of Haight-Ashbury and Flower Power. And Crystal was not really raised. She more or less grew up on her own without much adult guidance. She's very pretty though," Bella hurried to add.

"It was quite an experience," Prentice said drily. "Quite an education. We were very glad to get back to Salem, I can tell you that."

"So you have two grandchildren," Nell said, summarizing. "Martha and Michael."

"Quite correct. And we now have three great-grandchildren," Prentice said, "and all three of them have outlandish names. One is Brittany! That's a part of France. I was there in the war. She is Martha's daughter. Then there are Michael's offspring. The young man charged with carrying on the Eton name is himself named Derek, which I believe is some kind of rig in the oil drilling business. And the daughter is Indigo. That's a color isn't it?"

"It's the color of blue jeans," Arabella supplied. "But I'm not the one to comment on their names. I was landed with Arabella, for goodness' sake."

"Arabella," Prentice informed her, "is a family name. There are Arabellas on your family tree going back four generations."

Arabella rolled her eyes at Nell.

Henny came into the dining room and stood at Prentice's elbow looking down at his plate.

"You've hardly touched your lunch, Tice." Her tone accused.

"I've been too busy talking, Henny. I'm sorry, especially since you've prepared such delicious food."

Nell picked up the theme. "Yes, delicious is the word. The mushroom broth was excellent."

"Bella made that," Henny told her. "It's one of her specialties."

Nell looked at her hostess in such surprise that Arabella laughed.

"I love to cook," she said, "and when Henny and I are in the kitchen together—up to our elbows in some concoction—well, those are the best times, aren't they Henny?"

The two women shared an affectionate look.

"Henny's been looking after us for...what is it? Twenty-eight years now?"

"That's right." Henny shot Tice a look of mock fierceness. "And some of those times have been very trying!"

He laughed. "I'll redeem myself at supper, Henny." Then Prentice Eton shifted expression. He looked directly at Nell. "Now I'll come to the point, Nell. You must be wondering why you were subjected to this long saga. Bella and I realize that our grandchildren—but especially our great-grandchildren—

do not know much about their family. About their forebears. And in this omission, we fear we have let our family down. We intend to rectify that. We want these young folks to know the sort of people they came from. Moreover, each stands to inherit not inconsiderable wealth, and we wish them to understand the responsibility and obligations that come with this wealth.

He paused to take a sip of water.

"We have asked Robert here to find someone to help us write our memoir—a joint memoir actually. A memoir that will detail the families each of us came from as well as the family values that have informed our lives. Robert has told us there is only one writer he could possibly recommend. That is you, Nell Bane. What do you say? Will you accept us as clients?"

Chapter 3

The Hawthorne Inn sat on the Common's south side and the windows of its tavern room received the western light of afternoon—a light that made the red-gold wood glow. Robert had suggested a post-meeting wrap-up, and Nell was grateful for his willingness to help her process the impressions from the Etons' luncheon.

"I've always been fond of this place," Nell said, looking about her. The room made her happy. "Except the last time I was here at the Hawthorne it was for that terrible testimonial dinner for Deke Kernow."

She shuddered, remembering the celebration lauding a client who proved to be a complete phony.

"Then we will drink to the present," Robert smiled. "And to new clients who are blue-blooded and true."

He had ordered Dubonnet cocktails for them both and he lifted his glass.

"Amen," said Nell.

"Well, what do you think?" he asked, getting right to

business.

"I think," Nell said slowly, "that Prentice and Arabella are both delightful. I like them. I liked them immediately. And for some reason I trust them. I'm a little unsure though how this double memoir could work."

She fell silent, turning the cocktail glass between her hands, making the ice cubes chink and staring into the ruby depths.

Robert waited.

"Huh," she said finally, as if responding to an unheard voice. "Well, yes... that could work."

Nell thought further, her eyes now looking at some distant point far from the Tavern on the Green. But she returned suddenly and locked onto Robert's gaze.

"I'd probably have to charge more for a two-fer."

"My dear Nell, don't look so stricken. Of course you'd charge more for a double memoir. The Etons wouldn't expect you to do less. And believe me, my dear, they can afford your price and will be happy to pay it. So think about working up an estimate, and we'll discuss it with Tice and Bella. And I think you should begin work very quickly. I know they are eager to have this memoir and to present it to their great-grandchildren. Not to be coarse, but time is not on their side."

Chapter 4

Nell had her head in the freezer when her neighbor, Bunty Whitney, pushed through the back door, knocking as she came.

"What're you looking for?"

"Beef stock. Consommé. I had a marvelous mushroom broth yesterday and I can't wait to try the recipe."

"I thought you were going to Salem. To see those—you know—older people. They served you mushroom soup?"

"Mushroom *broth*. There's a difference. Say mushroom soup and you think of a grey-brown sludge in a bowl. Broth is light and delicate."

"*Broth*, then," said Bunty sourly, "fine. But did you get the job?"

"It's mine if I want it."

"Do you?"

"It'll have its challenges, but I'm planning to take them on."

"Good," said Bunty.

"Why good?"

"I'm developing an interest in the characters you pick up as clients," Bunty said. "Now that I'm out of the psychotherapy racket, I find I like to hear about the sick-tickets still prowling around out there."

"Bunty! None of my clients have been sick tickets!"

"No?" Bunty raised an eyebrow.

"Well," Nell hedged "Maybe Deke Kernow was a little...unusual..."

"Unusual? He was phony as a thirteen dollar bill." Bunty's quirked eyebrow went a notch higher. "And how 'bout the lovely Angela? She who was arrested on attempted murder charges?"

"Oh," Nell said humbly. "Well."

She thought, then offered brightly, "Andrew Povitch was okay though."

"Point taken," Bunty acknowledged. "Now tell me about this mushroom *broth*."

Nell indicated the handwritten recipe on the counter.

"Rapeseed oil," said Bunty, peering at the recipe. "What the hell is that? And truffle oil for god's sake! What are these people? Millionaires?"

"Yes," said Nell matter-of-factly. "They are. Do you suppose I need to use rapeseed oil? Could I substitute olive oil, d'you think?"

Bunty shrugged.

"I'd be the last person to ask. I would be willing to taste this mushroom broth though. Can I invite myself to stay for supper?"

Nell laughed. "Of course. I love guinea pigs."

ARABELLA ETON'S MUSHROOM BROTH
2 T rapeseed oil
1 medium onion sliced

1 garlic clove crushed
75ml Madeira or sherry
4 cups hot beef consommé or beef stock
1 lb mixed mushroom, cleaned and very thinly sliced
A grating of fresh nutmeg
Leaves from a large sprig of thyme
Truffle oil for drizzling

Arabella apparently heated the oil in large pan and gently cooked the onion until it was soft and golden brown. Then she'd add the garlic and cook it gently. Next the Madeira, which she'd reduce by two-thirds before adding the hot consommé, mushrooms, nutmeg and thyme. Finally she would season the broth and bring to boil, then cover it and simmer for 15-20 till mushrooms were tender, then serve the broth in warmed bowls with the truffle oil drizzle.

Chapter 5

The Etons accepted Nell's proposal to ghostwrite their double memoir with few questions and no quibbling over costs. And Prentice promptly produced a check for the first third of the writing job.

"Now if you find you are exceeding your estimated time," he said as he handed it over, "you are to speak up and we'll make the necessary adjustments."

"I appreciate that very much," Nell told him, "but I believe I've included some contingency in my estimate. I think we'll come pretty close."

She smiled.

"And I'm ready to begin work whenever you and Arabella say the word."

"Then what is the drill?" Prentice asked crisply.

Nell could suddenly see the successful businessman he had been.

"I think we'll begin at the beginning," Nell said. "No, don't smile. It isn't that obvious. Sometimes I start with a significant event, then go back to an earlier time and backfill. But in this case I'd like you, Prentice, and next you, Arabella, to tell me the individual stories of your family backgrounds. Also the stories of your childhoods. I'd like to know the experiences and influences that shaped you into the people you've become. I will record your stories on this."

Nell displayed her small Sony digital recorder.

"I may ask you a few questions during the sessions, but I usually don't like to interrupt the flow."

Nell looked at each of the Etons in turn. This ghostwriting business was new to them and she wanted to be certain they would understand the process.

"A session won't exceed two hours," she continued. "That's as much information as I can manage without getting super-saturated. I'll go home to Newburyport and listen to the recordings—usually several times through. Then I'll begin to write. I will find your individual voices and make every effort to write as you would speak. But part of the reason you have a professional writer doing this is be sure of cogency and economies of word. As we go along, I'll share drafts with you so you can see how the memoir—excuse me—memoirs are progressing, and this will give you the opportunity to catch mistakes or voice your approvals or disapprovals."

Once again Nell paused and searched her new clients' faces and saw only alert interest.

"I can't wait to begin," Arabella said. "Isn't this exciting, Tice?"

In answer, her husband smiled at her.

"We'll be learning new things, my dear, and yes, it is exciting."

Chapter 6

"This is a lovely house," Nell said as she met her appointment for the first memoir session. Arabella had led her into the living room where Prentice's wheelchair was parked near the front windows, then she had discretely withdrawn.

"You have lived here a long while, I assume," she said to Tice.

"My whole life," Prentice smiled. "In fact, I was born upstairs—the second bedroom on the left. But there haven't always been Etons in this house. My father purchased the place shortly after he and my mother were married. They were living down on Derby Street then, just a few steps from the Customs House, as a matter of fact. I believe my father thought the area was becoming too busy. Too commercial. So he selected this house with its view of the Common where he envisioned his children-to-be would be at play."

"And did you? Play on the Common?"

"Oh, of course. When my brother and I were small, we felt like we could run forever here."

"I want to hear what life was like for you then," Nell said. "Because your great-grandchildren will want to know what life was like in the early days of the twentieth century, little details of ordinary, everyday living will help make you and your life real for them. For example, did you sneak into the kitchen to rob the cookie jar? What foods did you hate? What were Sundays like in this house?"

Nell paused to see if Prentice was getting this and was pleased to see that he was nodding. A distant smile was playing across his face.

"Stories evolve in circles," she continued. "They meander. They don't move in straight lines. So I have learned to listen in circles, and together, we must be patient with them—with the stories—and allow them to take us where they please."

She removed her notebook and the Sony from her briefcase and prepared for business, but Prentice first needed to be sure she was comfortable.

"Would you like something to drink, my dear? Water? Tea? I can send for Henny. I'd trot out to the kitchen myself, but since the stroke four years ago, I can no longer trot."

He looked rueful. Nell sympathized.

"Do you find the restriction frustrating?"

The old man sighed.

"Not as much as you'd think probably. I am fortunate to have Frank—Frank Largent. He was our caretaker, handyman and general Mister Fix-It for years, and when I crumpled, he stepped up to act as personal assistant. So we carry on. Now about that drink..."

But Nell was not thirsty and she was eager to begin.

"Tell me stories, Mr. Eton. I want to hear all about your early years."

Chapter 7

It took several visits to North Federal Street for Nell to collect the stories of Prentice's early years. She didn't want to move onto the work with Arabella until she felt she really knew Prentice Eton, who, after the first two sessions suggested she call him Tice.

"After all, my dear, you know—or soon will know—some of my most intimate biographical facts. We can hardly be at arms' length. My closest friends and family call me Tice. I'd like you to do so as well."

Patterns were starting to be revealed. Nell became familiar with the two generations that had preceded Tice and informed his personality and values. Finally she was able to being writing the story of his early years.

Excerpts from
The Early Years
Prentice Eton

We lived by a routine, it seemed. Everything was measured and predictable, and for a child, I think, this is beneficial. Life on North Federal Square was orderly and ordered. I generally knew—and could depend upon—what would happen next; I understood what was expected of me, and therefore, I knew who I was. I was an Eton. I was Prentice Eton, named for my paternal grandfather. And I was a son of George and Daisy Spofford Eton who were, respectively, the children of Prentice and Mary Snow Eton on one side and on the other of Willard and Charlotte Gray Spofford.

At Thanksgiving and Christmas, the dining room table was fitted with all its leaves and Etons and Spoffords lined both sides. Then, gradually, and one-by-one, the oldest generation left us until finally, only Grandmother Charlotte Spofford remained. She was always seated on my father's left in the place of honor, and she was as deaf as the granite steps out front. She demanded that everything be repeated twice or even three times until she understood it. Or thought she had. Furthermore, she blamed her hearing loss on the rest of us, accusing us of speaking too softly or of mumbling. As a result, the dinner conversation sounded something like this:

"I said," Pa would bray, "Would you care for another slice of turkey, Mother?"

"What was that? Speak distinctly, George."

"Turkey. I asked about turkey."

"Key? Have you lost a key? Or were you asking me about gravy? Really, George, you do mumble dreadfully."

My brother Willard and I and our little sister Caroline were seated at the table's center and it was all we could do not to giggle. It would have been very bad manners to giggle at Grandmother, so we sucked the insides of our cheeks together and tried to look straight ahead and not at each other. And we never took a sip of milk or water while one of these conversations was carrying on. That would put you in danger of laughing and blowing milk out your nose. Thanksgiving and Christmas and Sundays too—it was all very much the same. Tradition. It was one of the things that made us Etons.

# # #

There was a routine to each year. Willard and I went to school, of course—to the Holmes School, which we understood we'd attend through the eighth grade. Then we knew we would start at Phillips Andover. We'd have to board there because in those days, the round trip from Salem to Andover would be too long to undertake twice each day, but Mother assured us we would be home on weekends.

In school, I loved math—arithmetic, we called it—and I hated spelling and Latin. I liked English because it was like the stories Mother read to us and because grammar reminded me of arithmetic. There were rules. You just had to learn them and follow them.

Willard and I played on the Common in all weather. There were no hills for sledding, but there was plenty of space for games of fox-and-geese and snow fort building. We had tremendous snowball fights. Real battles.

As we got a little older, we played down by the harbor. We weren't supposed to go out on the jetty—Mother was a worrier—but we often did. We knew we wouldn't fall in. We were saltwater kids. In the cold part of the year we had Salem Harbor to explore and play around and its fascination for us was always fresh. But in the summers, we had the best of it. We had the coast of Maine and The Rocks.

The Etons had a house at Goose Rocks. The Rocks—a big, old gray-shingled monster, all salt-stained and the trim was freshened with white paint every spring. There were vast attics for playing in on rainy days and wrap-around porches with white-painted rocking chairs that squeaked endlessly on the floorboards. You can't imagine what a relief it was to run up on that porch after playing for hours on the beach and in the water. Suddenly there were cool boards under our bare feet and a pitcher of lemonade on a table. Beads of moisture running down its sides. Tall glasses on a tray. The cool blue-painted roof overhead instead of the searing sun.

# # #

It was the summer I was ten and my brother Willard was twelve. Our little sister Caroline had just turned six, and it happened this way. This is the first time I remember enduring a life-changing event. I had a nasty summer cold and my mother forbade me from going out in the skiff with Willard.

"You stay indoors, Tice," she said, "You don't and that cold'll just get worse. Nip it in the bud. Keep yourself indoors and tomorrow we'll see if you're well enough to run around. No bare feet though!"

Gosh, I was hornet-mad! Mad at Mother. Mad at the cold. Even mad at Willard who didn't have a summer cold and who grinned at me as if to say "Baby" and off he went to the boathouse to get gear for the *Goose*.

The *Rocky Goose*. We bought the skiff secondhand off an old fella who'd built 'er himself. Willard and I saved up all the winter to buy her. She'd been called *Gull*, but we painted the name out and rechristened her *Rocky Goose* which we thought was terribly funny—a witty play on the name Goose Rocks and a reference to the skiff's instability. She pitched and rolled something wicked when a wave hit broadside, but we thought she was terrific. We'd just grab onto the gunwales and whoop and yell and ride out the rocking. We pinched a bottle of beer out of the gardener's shed and cracked it over *Goosie's* bow to christen her properly.

So off went Willard that morning, and there was I. Indoors.

Well, we had hundreds of old books at The Rocks and they all smelled of damp, but I didn't care. I loved that smell. It was the smell of summer and of the ocean and of that big old camp far from schoolrooms. It was The Rocks's own peculiar smell. I was reading *The Leatherstocking Saga* that summer and was in the middle of *The Deerslayer* but I couldn't keep my mind on Natty Bumppo that day. All I could think about was Willard out in the skiff—free as a seagull—and here was I, made to stay behind like a baby. I was furious at my mother.

It was sundown when they found the *Rocky Goose* hullside up, but it was sunrise before they found Willard.

I don't remember another blessed thing until I was sitting in a pew in that Congregational church on Kennebunkport's backside. That I remember. The heat that August day was terrific and I think it blistered the next impressions into my memory. The air was stifling. My cold was better but I kept having to fight the urge to cough and a huge bluebottle was bumping-bumping-bumping against the window glass, then buzzing furiously when it couldn't get out in the fresh air.

At one point Caroline slid her hand into mine—her damp little hand—and she looked up at me with eyes full of misery and questions and I had this jolt—this epiphany—that I was the big brother now. The responsible one and I had to take care of Caroline who suddenly seemed like the most precious, the very dearest thing, in the world. In a moment's flash, I realized we were family with a special connection I couldn't name or even fathom, and I had an instant recognition of what all that meant. I can't explain it now. Can't put it into words but it has something to do with needing to take care. Protect. And it acknowledges how ineffably precious those ties are— precious and at the same time precarious. That day we buried Willard, everything changed for me.

The next day I took an axe to the hull of the *Rocky Goose*. I was bawling like a little kid who'd skinned both knees the whole time I tried to chop that wooden skiff into matchsticks. Pa had

Mr. Davies, the hired man, haul the skiff out back, finish the job and burn the wood. I think Pa was relieved to see the last of the damnable *Rocky Goose*.

Chapter 8

The sunroom, Nell decided, was Arabella Eton's sacred space.

Nell believed everyone had one. Or at least everyone should.

"Your sacred space?" Nell asked with a smile when her hostess led her into the sunroom.

Arabella Eton was surprised. "Why, yes, I think you could call it that."

The elderly woman gazed around the room as if seeing it afresh through Nell's eyes. Then she nodded vigorously.

"Yes. That's exactly what it is. I don't know why the room speaks so clearly to me though. Perhaps it's the light. The first light of morning is lovely, slanting at an angle across the Common, but the afternoon light has its own charm as well. It is more a reflected light—caught in the mirrors and windows that give back its own colors."

She turned to Nell with delight. "Thank you, my dear, for showing me something new about the room that I've long taken for granted. My sacred space. I'll remember that."

Nell settled with pleasure into one of the matching armchairs upholstered in a flowered and quilted chintz that somehow managed to be old-fashioned yet very up-to-date. Arabella took the matching chair directly opposite and leaned toward Nell across a small table between them.

"The first thing to settle is what you'll call me," she said. "I'd like you to call me Bella. It's what my friends call me and we will certainly become close friends. Arabella sounds like my grammar school teacher. Someone wearing a corset."

"I'd like that," Nell replied, "and you're right. We are going to be close while you share all your memories and your secret thoughts. And I hope you'll come to consider me a friend."

She smiled. "And so we'll begin."

Excerpts from
The Early Years
Arabella Whiteside Eton

Both my parents were preachers' kids. And in them, I suppose, some of the myths about preachers' kids were realized. Uncle Henry (on mother's side) for instance was a gambler who was known to bet on horses, but rarely on the winning ones, and his own father denounced him from the pulpit.

"While it pains me to say it," Grandfather Dowd is supposed to have thundered, "my own flesh and blood is no better than the gamblers Jesus turned out of the temple!"

Grandfather Dowd was a Congregational minister who for years stood at the helm of one of the most famous pulpits in Boston. The grandfather on my father's side—the Reverend Dr. Charles Wilson Whiteside—was a Dean of the Harvard Divinity School and an Episcopalian.

Thus, in my parents' marriage, two great New England Protestant theologies came together with a genteel clash, and the patriarchs on both sides warily watched the offspring for signs of apostasy. But there wasn't so much as a breath of scandal in the John Whiteside family that was created when my mother and father took marriage vows—in, I might add, a Congregational church. Both my parents were sober, upstanding citizens who raised three daughters to be God-fearing, baked-bean-and-brown-bread New Englanders. There was no repetition of Uncle Henry's more unfortunate proclivities.

Grandfather Whiteside had been dead for some years by the time Sybil, Martha and I bloomed upon John Whiteside's branch of the family tree. Grandfather Dowd, however, was still around to scrutinize his granddaughters for signs of Papist tendencies.

"Papa Whiteside wasn't that sort of Episcopalian," Mama kept telling her father, but it amused Grandfather to pretend that he had been.

While we did not know our Grandfather Whiteside, we had much reason to thank him, for he left a legacy that my sisters and I treasured above everything else. In the eighteen-eighties, the Rev. Dr. Whiteside participated in the great Episcopal land purchase on New Hampshire's Squam Lake. Around that time, a number of ministers and faculty from the Divinity School bought significant parcels of land on the western side of the lake, and they formed quite an active summer colony that included the establishment of a summer chapel—St. Peter's On-the-Mount—and an outdoor chapel on Chocorua Island that came to be known as Church Island. Grandfather's seventy-eight acre parcel was just a little ways beyond the village of Holderness and it featured a wide peninsula that pointed down into the lake. Toward the end of this finger, Grandfather built a big rambling camp, in the style of the times and the area. With obvious plans for future development, he named it Main Camp. In time it came to be known simply as Mains. As his children married, Grandfather Whiteside built each couple their own camp as a wedding present, and over time, four rambling, shingle camps surrounded Mains: Eastwind, Westwind, Southwind, and Northwind. My father was the first child to marry and our camp was Eastwind. Eventually Uncles David and Charles moved their new families into Westwind and Northwind and Aunt Edith and Uncle Daniel Burleigh had Southwind. Aunt Elsie, who never married, was to inherit Mains.

Memorial Day sounded the retreat to Camp. With noises of parades passing on nearby Beacon Street, all the celebration and activity in our house on Pinckney Street was focused on packing. The maids would be hurrying back and forth, feeding stacks of clothing into the gapping jaws of the great trunks, and Mama carried long lists everywhere she went, endlessly checking and rechecking and growing quite frazzled with all the pressure and preparation. Finally, we would board the train and travel deep into New Hampshire as far as Plymouth. Then we'd go by farm wagon from the depot to Camp.

The summer escape was a huge undertaking. Besides the trunks and other accouterments, there were Mama, me, Sybil and Martha as well as two or three Irish serving girls who were as excited as we were to be escaping Boston for the season and to seeing summer friends once again. I suppose for the girls it was Bridget and Tom and Kathleen. For us it was our Eton and Burleigh cousins and friends from other camps along the lake like the Galbraith children and the Thurstons and the farm kids from across the road.

As evenings closed in at Camp, we played endless games of Hide-and-Seek and Prisoner's Base. We raced through the darkening woods where there was always the threat of tripping on a root or stubbing a toe into a chuck of granite. We dodged places where we knew poison ivy grew and swatted at mosquitos, and it would be long after dark before someone's mother began calling her children in. Mama had a cowbell and when we heard it clanging away, Syb and Martha and I knew we had to scamper or we'd be grounded the next night and banned from games. I remember one time when I was made to stay inside and had to listen to the hoots and calls and laughter from the woods. I felt so isolated and left out that I never ignored that cowbell again! By day's light the next morning, the same gang of kids would be together again in the lake—splashing and paddling canoes and baiting hooks on the ends of bamboo poles.

Papa came up to Camp by train most weekends, and then on Monday mornings, Albert Day took him to Holderness in the launch to catch a wagon to the depot. This trip to Holderness was a treat that my sisters and I begged to share.

It would be just past dawn when Papa in his business suit and straw hat walked down to the dock where Albert Day had the launch waiting. Albert Day had placed the porridge board across the gunwales and one of the Irish girls carried down a tray with three bowls of oatmeal and set the bowls into holes drilled in the board—each hole the perfect size to hold a bowl of oatmeal. Then Albert Day would cast off and down the lake we'd go with Papa in the stern looking splendid in his city suit. As well, we carried the huge straw laundry trunk, tagged, and also bound for Boston where the clothes and sheets would be laundered and sent back the next week.

As Albert Day guided the boat, we three little girls sat in the bottom, eating our oatmeal. The launch sat low, so the water was up around the hull and it was like being in a bathtub, except the water was cool under our bottoms instead of warm. The early morning mist would be rising from the water. The loons would be calling. And the blueberry bushes draping over the rocks along the edge of the lake would be soaked with dew, and we'd look for diamonds.

"There's one!" we'd cry when an early sunbeam shot across the lake and struck a bead of water in just the right way.

"I saw it first!" Martha, the littlest, would cry.

"Did not," Sybil or I would tell her.

"I did so! Didn't I Albert Day? Tell them I did so!"

"Girls, girls," Papa would say, "Albert, are those bass in the cove ever going to start biting d'you think?"

"They should have been biting by now, I'd wager. Even 'fore this. I don't know what's the matter with the damn bass this season. 'Scuse the language, sir. Awful sorry, in front of the little girls and all."

"Don't worry about it Albert. They're eating their breakfasts and they're not paying attention anyhow."

And we'd giggle.

Then the launch would bump against the dock and Albert Day would say,

"Have a fine day, sir," as Papa stepped up onto the dock.

And we girls like three baby robins in a nest would pipe, "Good- bye Papa! We love you Papa! See you on Friday, Papa!"

Those impressions are still so vivid to me. And I'd feel so sorry for any child who couldn't spend summers in New Hampshire where the air smelled of sun-warmed pine needles and sweet fern...where you'd bend and pinch a leaf of wintergreen, then chew it to release is cool flavor, then spit out the chewed leaf when it turned sour...where you'd pluck a long blade of coarse grass, hold it tight between your thumbs and blow it like a whistle. Most of the year it was Pinckney Street and Miss Winsor's classrooms and dancing lessons in a ballroom that was big but also unaccountably stuffy. But summer could balance all that. Cancel it out. I lived for summer and for Camp.

Chapter 9

"Bella," Prentice complained, "you began your story with a rather impertinent observation about preachers' kids. Wouldn't it have been better to lead off with an explanation of exactly who your grandfathers were? That they were both highly respected theologians?"

Nell, who was the real culprit in determining the style of Arabella's narration, held her breath, waiting.

"Tice," said Arabella spiritedly, "you are a stuffy old bore! This isn't an eighth grade essay! You or I could write a stuffy old essay. We've hired young Nell Bane here to write a memoir our Grands and Greats will want to read. We don't want them tossing the book aside because it starts out with a genealogy straight out of Genesis! They'd be yawning from the get-go. We want to catch their interests. Entice them to read on. And I believe that in this opening, Nell has done exactly that. She has gone to the very navel of my narration and caught up— the way you'd catch with a crochet hook—the fragile, lively thread of the story. I think it's perfect! You do as you wish with your narration—that was our understanding—and I'll do as I like with mine!"

Nell, her eyebrows raised, exchanged a look with Prentice. His expression was startled for a few moments. More startled by Bella's spirited retort than by what she said. Then he grinned.

"By Jove, Arabella, you are right!" Then he looked at Nell. "That's the girl I married and now you can see why I married her!"

He laughed. An astounding laugh that seemed like it had come from a man much more robust than he. Nell was relieved.

"Well, with that detail sorted out, what other comments do you have?" Nell asked.

"I see that you start many sentences with conjunctions," Arabella observed primly. "I was taught that was not proper."

Nell smiled.

"Once you know all the rules, you're free to break some of them," she said. "I try to write the way people actually talk. We don't usually speak in whole sentences but in fragments. And we often begin new thoughts with conjunctions or omit a proper subject altogether in violation of the 'every sentence should have a subject and a predicate' rule."

She shrugged.

"I can change those things if you wish and abide rigidly by the rules of grammar, but the trade-off is a compromised style. Your memoir will be stiff and somewhat awkward. Before I began writing, I studied your speaking style—both of your styles. I listened to your unique voices and that is what I have tried to put on paper."

Both Etons were listening attentively.

"Light begins to dawn," Arabella said. "Well, for my 'voice' in this memoir, I want my voice to be heard. How do you feel, Tice?"

He was thoughtful. Then he too nodded with conviction.

"In looking at the two drafts side by side," he said, "I see they are different. Individual. It wouldn't do, would it, to have us sound like identical twins? We may have hired a ghostwriter, but I see that it is important for who we are as individuals come through."

"Thank you," said Nell. "Your reactions to these first drafts are especially important. Now that you've approved them, subsequent drafts will proceed quite easily, I think. We'll add more to 'The Early Years', then we'll go on to 'The War Years'."

Chapter 10

"I've never talked much about the war," Tice said thoughtfully. "Most of us didn't. Those who'd come out alive—some of us in one piece and some with broken places—we just wanted to put the war behind us and get on with it. Even if we couldn't pick up our lives where we'd left them, we intended to try. So these locked-away memories that I will attempt to revisit may be difficult to disinter and perhaps even more difficult to revisit. But I will try."

And so Nell positioned the Sony as close to Prentice Eton as she dared, fearing that the old man's voice might grow weak or would falter during the long session she anticipated where he recalled and recounted those terribly difficult years of World War II. She switched the recorder on and settled back in her own chair to listen to the story.

Excerpt from
The War Years
Prentice Eton

I went in early. We had distant relatives and close friends in England—in Lincoln and Coventry and London—and the letters coming from over there were alarming, filled with descriptions of shortages and rationing and fears for the children exposed to the Blitz. They weren't complaining, mind you. That I remember well. They were just reporting in these very even tones on what was happening. My parents were terribly concerned and would hurry to the radio each evening before supper to hear the news. I was at Harvard then, but I came home. That's where I wanted to be—home with the family. My father would drop the newspaper—he still read *The Boston Evening Transcript* in those days—and he'd drop it beside his chair and tune in the big Philco. And my mother inevitably had her knitting needles going. She was knitting sweaters for the children of a niece in Lincoln. So even before Winston Churchill made his westward look the land is bright speech, I saw it coming. It was inevitable. Unstoppable. And just before Christmas in 1940, I went in.

I left behind a beautiful young woman named Arabella Whiteside. We'd talked of marriage, and I think Arabella was willing, but I didn't feel it was morally responsible to marry a young woman right before marching off to war where there was no guarantee that I'd come back to her. Or at any rate, that I'd come back as the man she'd married.

There was basic training, of course, then Officer Candidate School and before I had a chance to catch my breath I found myself at Fort Benning learning about tanks from the best of all tank commanders—George S. Patton, Jr. I was a cog in the wheel of "Hell on Wheels"—an outfit that was part of the 2nd Armored Division.

Patton had been promoted to brigadier general and made acting division commander of the 2nd Armored Brigade, 2nd Armored Division, and "Old Blood and Guts" was starting to make a big name for himself staging mass-exercises in Georgia and Florida. I felt fortunate to be a second lieutenant in his brigade. For the next months we stoodged all around the southeastern United States on various exercises—maneuvers in Tennessee, in Carolina, in Shreveport, Louisiana. But for us—for me—the real war finally began when we joined the Western Task Force of Operation Torch and landed at Casablanca. It was the 8th of November 1942.

For whatever reasons, the brass bumped me up to first lieutenant and eventually to captain. Captain Prentice Eton— that was something. I had a number of men under my command, and that meant I was responsible for the lives and souls of these people. That was a very sobering consideration, and as I consider it now, I was young to be in that position. But we were all young. You have to be young to do this kind of work. You have to believe you are immortal. Well, we were young, we were at war, and we were living and fighting under dangerous conditions in vehicles that were themselves deadly.

An M-4 Sherman tank is built like a rhinoceros. And it's bigger than a rhinoceros and like a rhino, it is heavily armor-plated. You'd think one of these monsters would offer all kinds of protection to its crew, and indeed, an infantryman who sees one rolling and bumping toward him, firing as it comes, would be correct in feeling terrified. But deadly doesn't just apply to a tank's outside, it applies to the inside too. Shells can pierce that hull and within seconds a tank's insides can be a coffin for the crew. Hatches jam, cabins fill with smoke, and fire can turn a tank into an incinerator. And even if the crew manages an escape, they are often escaping into heavy artillery fire.

Five men make a tank crew. There's the tank commander, the driver, assistant driver, a loader and a gunner. Wilbur Caldecott was a tank commander—the best one I ever knew and a finer man would be difficult to find. Spike Caldecott. I knew him from Phillips Andover and he never wanted to be a war room soldier. He wanted to be in the thick of it. He wanted to be inside an M-4, so I guess he was where he wanted to be when a shell came through the hide of his tank and killed him on the spot. The DNA of Spike Caldecott was splattered over every inch of the cabin and the rest of the crew. A man is never the same after an experience like that—after losing a friend like that.

During the war, the 2nd Armored Division did a lot of travelling. In July of '43 we were part of Operation Husky with the Western Task Force, and supported the 1st infantry at the Amphibious Battle of Gela. After that it was the second landing at Licata, Sicily, and from there we fought on to Palermo. We lost some tanks in that effort. Some tanks and some very good men. I saw one tank go into a bomb crater. The crew managed to escape through the back hatch only to be gunned down by artillery. One kid, a Boston kid named Mickey Shea, grabbed hold of the loader and half-carried, half-dragged him toward cover. He just about made it too. He would have made it if he hadn't grabbed Joe Gresick and tried to drag him to safety. But Mickey and Joe were buddies. Leaving him wasn't an option. I wrote to Mickey's family. Actually I wrote to Joe's too.

Those letters were hard to write, but I found solace in writing them. I had some notion how important those letters would be to the men's families, but the thing for me was in making each soldier come alive, to think of one or two very personal things about him and write about those.

In that battle where we lost Mickey Shea and Joe Gresick, I picked up some shrapnel myself. Infection set in and I spent a respite of sorts in an Army field hospital, hating every minute of the rest and chafing to get back to my unit.

#

By the spring of 1944 I was back and word came down that we would be hitting the beaches of Normandy by early June. When I think back now to that invasion...well...to the audacious concept of it! To the notion that an undertaking so complex and so massive could be successful, the hairs stand up on my arms. And even when we were concentrating on the miniscule and dangerous tasks that each of us had to play in the event, even then I was aware on some level that I was a part of something much, much greater.

We landed on the 9th of June under the command of Major Ed Brooks, and from Normandy we kept right on chewing. We chewed and fought as far as the Contentin Peninsula and eventually became part of the Operation Cobra assault, forming the right flank of the maneuver. The Germans attacked Avranches and we engaged them there. We were with the Third Army by this time and we tore through France, got to the Albert Canal in Belgium by early September and headed for the German border. There were skirmishes along the way. And there were snipers too. Deserters from the German army as well as German and Polish refugees were streaming west. The roads were thick with refugees and animals and the sky was busy too. Bombers whined overhead like swarms of hornets and the pilots would recognize us and waggle their wings as flew over.

The 2nd went on to Gellenkirchen, ultimately to launch an attack on the Seigfried Line, but as we were breaking through prior to crossing the Wurm River, the division and I parted company. I took another dose of shrapnel and also shattered my left leg. I was lucky again. The medics got to me and hauled me off to a field hospital. This time there was no return. My days as a cog in "Hell on Wheels" were over. I was shipped out.

There was some rehabilitation in England and by Christmas 1944 I was back in Salem, Massachusetts, ready to put the war—my war—behind me and start my new life.

Chapter 11

"It all seems so long ago," Bella Eton said. A memory—perhaps a haunting—clouded her face for a few moments. Nell waited. Then the memory seemed to lift and Bella's face relaxed. She composed herself and straightened her shoulders, then leaned back in her armchair and was able to smile at Nell.

"Well, nothing better to do than get on with it," she said cheerfully.

Nell hesitated. "You're up to this? You're sure?"

"Oh yes," Bella assured her. "It's all so long ago now. I can look back with assurance, if not clarity."

Her smile was confident. Nell wondered if it were sincere.

Excerpt from
The War Years
Arabella Whiteside Eton

For me, that period we call the war years moved so slowly that time scarcely seemed to pass at all. I was in love. I was in love with Prentice Eton and I wanted nothing so much as to be with him and to be Mrs. Prentice Eton. He had asked me to marry him and indeed, we talked of marrying before he went into the service, but reason—I suppose it was reason—prevailed. Tice was concerned that I might be a widow at age twenty. I think my biggest concern was that there wasn't time to plan the wedding of my dreams—a white gown with a train and eight bridesmaids. A wedding that involved choosing the invitations at Shreve's and arranging the wedding gifts on organdy-skirted tables in the library at Pinckney Street.

Well, I was young and hadn't yet developed the sense of social responsibility.

But I was in love and I wrote letters to Tice every day. Sometimes, if I was feeling especially bereft, I wrote twice a day. And I read his letters until I learned each by heart. He was busy and didn't have time to write everyday, and he explained he wouldn't have that much to say even if he did write. But oh, the letters that did arrive were read so many times the stationary grew soft as facial tissue. I'd lie on my back on my bed and read them over and over and tears would leak out of the corners of my eyes and into my hair, I missed him so.

And I have his letters still. Faded, they are, but they're tied up with pale blue ribbon and kept in a box in my dresser.

When he left, I continued to go to classes at Wellesley. I liked college well enough but it seemed—I don't know—kind of lame after you'd said goodbye to the man you loved and didn't know if that were the last goodbye you'd ever say.

# # #

One day in spring I came across a group of children playing croquet in Tower Court. Their high voices were British and I stopped to watch them play. I knew they were evacuees who had arrived at Wellesley College from Canada—part of a program organized by the Children's Oversees Reception Board. The idea was that the English families would send the children oversees to protect them from the terrible bombings in London and other cities and the children would live with Canadian and American families until it was safe to go home. Watching them, I thought how wrenching it must be for those parents and children to be parted so hurriedly. Devastating to have the children sent off into the unknown. They had to travel on ships and then be sorted into divisions or groups, some to stay in Canada and others to be shipped on to the States—to Wellesley—until they could be sorted again and claimed by kind strangers—Americans—who would shelter them for however long this awful war would last.

As I watched, I noticed a little girl sitting off to the side not playing croquet, but sadly plucking bits of grass. Her fingers were never still and I went to sit beside her and told her my name was Bella.

She was Olivia Cameron, she said. She was a shy child and she explained that she "just didn't feel up to playing croquet, thank you."

As we talked, I learned that her father had been called up in the Royal Navy Volunteer Reserve and that her mother and grandmother had decided she and her younger brother Julian would be safer abroad. She told me about seeing the barrage balloons on the way to Liverpool, then boarding the *Duchess of Athol* and holding the hand of her seven-year-old brother. They had both been weeping although trying not to, but Mummy and Granny were weeping also. There had been a fear of U-boats during the crossing, but they'd had a safe arrival in Canada, then a train ride to Wellesley and "well...here we are."

"What's next for you?" I asked.

"I don't know," Olivia admitted. "I believe someone will claim us—if they like the look of us, that is."

She seemed doubtful about this possibility.

"I hope that Julian and I can stay together. He is still small and he is so shy and I promised Mummy I'd look after him."

This responsibility appeared to be very heavy on the shoulders of this thin little girl of ten. And all at once I knew what I had to do!

I telephoned home and explained all this to Mama, who was brilliant—as I knew she would be—and she and my father made immediate arrangements to bring the Camerons home to Pinckney Street.

The letters from Europe were coming very erratically. Sometimes several months would pass with no word from Tice, then a thin packet of letters would arrive in a bundle. I still wrote every day but I'm afraid my letters were quite dull. I was just feeding words down an empty bin. I tried to be understanding, knowing that Tice wasn't always in a position to write. But my vivid imagination began to get the better of me. Finally I could stand it no longer. I thought if I had to eat another over-steamed Brussels sprout in the dormitory dining room or fill another blue book with an assigned essay or attend another class on Wordsworth, I'd go mad. I dropped out of Wellesley and signed up for a secretarial course at Katherine Gibbs.

I told my parents I was going to do war work—that it was my patriotic duty. They weren't pleased. A friend from summers at Squam—Betsy Galbraith—had moved to New York and was working in a typing pool accomplishing some sort of quasi-war-related job. She promised to get a position for me as soon as I learned to type fast enough to satisfy Katy Gibbs, and she offered to help me get a room near her at the Barbizon.

The Barbizon Hotel for Women was up on East 63rd. Very proper. Even Mama couldn't find fault. Men weren't allowed above the ground floor and there were strict codes for dress and conduct.

I told Betsy I'd get a taxi from Pennsylvania Station and to expect me. And Betsy was good as her word and did get me a position in a typing pool where I sat at a huge Royal for most of that hot summer, with big fans whirring and hundreds of keys clacking and the collars of all the girls going limp from sweat. Of course we didn't sweat—we daintily perspired.

Now, as well as letters to Tice, I wrote letters home to my family in Boston, and Mama was very good about writing to me in care of Betsy Galbraith at the Barbizon. But I came to dread her letters. Each one brought news of another friend who'd been harmed or killed in the war. Billy Hamilton killed in a mine explosion in Italy. Charlie Thurston, one of the boys from Camp who was Navy Air, was shot down in the Pacific on his second bombing run. Constance James, whom I'd known since nursery school, lost her brother and her fiancé in the same week. Each bulletin brought the war ominously closer, and I came to dread the sight of Mama's handwriting on an envelope.

I came home from New York in September at the very ragtag end of the summer. There was one long weekend when we managed to pool our ration cards for the gas to drive to Squam. Mama had spent the summer there with the Camerons and Martha who had a job at the local girls' camp. I couldn't believe the Camerons. Olivia and Julian had each grown taller and were tanned and eager to show me everything about Camp. They cannonballed off the dock. They dived deep into the lake and swam underwater and came up grinning onto Shelf Rock just as my sisters and I and our cousins used to do. There were still some younger cousins at Camp so games of Hide-and Seek still ranged in the woods at night and this time I was the one sitting on the screened porch listening to the calls and whispers in the night. Julian and Olivia went trotting through Mains, calling to Aunt Elsie that they were just visiting the cookie jar. I remembered when these children would have called them biscuits.

The Camerons lived with my family for four-and-a-half years, and when their parents were finally able to make the crossing to collect them and take them home to England, they found two, tall Americans with so many stories to tell. When the reunited family boarded the train for New York where their ship was waiting, there were tears again. Tears from all the Whitesides and tears from our two little Brits who would be family forever.

Then, toward the end of that terrible year, we got word that Tice was coming home.

Chapter 12

Nell was tired. And she admitted as much to Bunty Whitney.

"It was a hard row to hoe," she said, "getting the stories of the war years winkled out of the Etons. For one thing, it all happened so long ago, but distance aside, it seemed difficult for them in other ways." She paused and Bunty waited, listening. "Prentice explained at the start that he rarely spoke about his war service. That it was difficult to talk about the war. And that seems to be a feeling shared by most World War II veterans. They clammed up when they returned. Tried to carry on as brave soldiers right on into civilian life. I can certainly understand that, but Bella seemed restrained too."

Nell shook her head.

"I don't know...I just got the feeling she was holding something back. Something crucial."

She shook her head again, this time to clear it.

Bunty, who had been listening with a professional silence perfected during long sessions with her psychotherapy patients, finally spoke.

"Well, I know just the remedy you need. The pick-me-up."

She waited for Nell to turn with a quizzical gaze, then she slapped down her trump card.

"Soup!" she declared. "You must make some soup. Now tell me, what will it be?"

So Nell hauled out her cookbook of soup recipes and began randomly reading candidates to Bunty from the "M" section.

"Miso," Nell read. "Matzo ball, Meatball pizza..."

At each name, Nell looked up but Bunty's expression was impassive.

"Mock turtle," she continued.

"Heaven forfend!" Bunty muttered.

"If you say so," Nell commented. She read on: "Minestrone, Mulligatawny, Mediterranean chickpea..."

"Wait," said Bunty, "what was that—that mulligan thing? What is that?"

"Mulligatawny? It's an Indian-sort of soup. From India, I mean. It means pepper water and it has rice and curry. It's very good."

But Bunty was nodding.

"Yes, I'd like to try that."

So here's how Nell made the soup.

MULLIGATAWNY SOUP
1/2 cup chopped onion
2 stalks celery, chopped
1 carrot, diced
1/4 cup butter
1-1/2 tablespoons all-purpose flour
1-1/2 teaspoons curry powder
4 cups chicken broth
1/2 apple, cored and chopped

1/4 cup white rice
1 skinless, boneless chicken breast half, cut into cubes
salt to taste
ground black pepper to taste
1 pinch dried thyme
1/2 cup heavy cream, heated

After she had gathered the ingredients, Nell sautéed the onions, celery, carrot, and butter in a large soup pot. Next she added the flour and curry, and cooked this for 5 minutes. Then in went the chicken stock and Nell mixed it well. She brought it to a boil and simmered it for a half hour. Finally it was time to add the apple, rice, chicken, salt, pepper, and thyme which required another bit of simmering—about 20 minutes worth to cook the rice to doneness. At last Nell added the hot cream just before she dished up a bowlful for Bunty.

"Namaste," she said, serving the soup with a slight bow.

"Can you really make mock turtle soup?" Bunty wanted to know.

Chapter 13

"So how are you getting on with Bella and Tice?" Robert Hutchins asked.

Robert was standing Nell to lunch at the Black Cow, and they were seated in Nell's favorite booth—the one that felt like a cabin on a lovely old sailboat. The window just beyond their elbows framed a view of the Merrimac River in full turbulence. It was raining hard and the gray river roiled and seethed and reversed itself, breaking into fractious eddies that seemed, to Nell, hungry to tear into any small craft that might risk the rain and tide.

She thought of Robert's drive up from Boston in the storm. It must have been a tedious ride, but Robert's black Mercedes would have floated along, hugging the wet road with only the soft sounds of swishing water on the roadway and the clearing beat of the wipers to interrupt the quiet.

"The Etons are lovely, both of them," Nell said. "I'm even becoming comfortable calling them Tice and Bella, and the double memoir seems to be steaming along at a great rate.

Why do you ask? Have you had comments from them?"

"I have," Robert replied, "and they couldn't be more pleased with you. I think they'll soon start viewing you as the daughter they no longer have."

"Oh dear," said Nell.

Robert was regarding her levelly.

"What's wrong?" she asked. "Have I something on my face?"

She dabbed at her chin and then at her cheek with the napkin.

"No," Robert shook his head. "But they are terribly eager to present the finished copies of the memoirs to the Greats."

"The great-grandchildren, you mean?"

"Yes. As distinguished from the Grands—grandchildren Michael Eton and Martha Baker. It is the Greats who are their hope—the ones who will carry the Etons' legacy forward. Tice and Bella don't know these young people at all, and they are planning to invite each one to visit individually. They hope to acquaint the Greats with Salem and Boston, to speak with them about family—that's Family in upper case—and finally, and with great ceremony, to present each with a hardbound copy of the memoir."

"You're handling the publication, aren't you?" asked Nell looking for confirmation.

"Yes. We'll do a print-on-demand run which will allow Tice and Bella to print as many copies, or as few, as they wish. It will also allow them to order more at any time."

Robert smiled.

"When I think back to the olden days—which were just a few years ago actually—this would never have been possible. Publishing has changed."

"Changed for the better?" Nell asked.

Since publishing had long been Robert Hutchins's

business, she was curious.

"On balance, yes," replied Robert. "There are compromises, of course. Certain corners have been cut. Perhaps there has been some deterioration in quality, but the new order has allowed many to write and publish books for their own limited distribution and pleasure. And that's a good thing. And, may I add, the new order has been very good for your ghostwriting business."

It was Nell's turn to smile. She tipped the lip of her wine glass against Robert's.

"To the new order," she said.

The waitress appeared with their starters. P.E.I mussels with shallots, garlic and white wine for Robert and clam chowder for Nell, who explained, with a nod toward the rain-streaked window, "This day calls for something warm and soothing."

"Now," said Robert Hutchins, as if picking up a conversational thread, "your work with the Etons isn't going to end with the publication of the memoir."

Nell looked up from the chowder.

Robert extracted a mussel from its shell and bathed it in the juices in the bottom of the bowl. Nell waited while he did this. She waited some more while he consumed the mussel.

"They are hoping—well, they very much want you to be part of the reception committee for the Greats. I am to be on the committee as well."

"For goodness sake why?"

"Apparently we will help bridge the generation gap. To use a line from an old song: it's a long, long way from May to December. Tice and Bella have the idea that the Greats will relate better to us than to their great-grandparents. Indigo, the youngest is only seventeen and Brittany, at twenty-two, is the eldest. Derek, at nineteen or twenty, is in the middle."

"It's been a long, long time since I was twenty-two," Nell pointed out drily. "Never mind seventeen."

"They expect to pay you for these services," Robert said. "Your time will be well compensated."

"Sort of like babysitting," Nell muttered.

"You have become an expert in all things Eton," Robert told her. "You have been privy to details and stories that didn't make it into the book. You have opinions and can explicate for these young people things about their family that Tice and Bella aren't able to share. Think of this mission as an extension of your ghostwriting."

Salads arrived and the starter dishes removed. Robert Hutchins, preparing to tuck into a Caesar salad, changed the subject.

"Did I tell you what Jerry is up to these days? He has a new assignment. He's been invited to do a room in a Designer Showhouse in Newton. He's fairly vibrating with ideas, and he wants us both there for the opening. And by the way, how is your friend Bunty Whitney?"

And Nell knew there was nothing more to be said about the Etons' plans for the Greats.

Chapter 14

"Halfway," Nell said aloud to herself. "Halfway through the memoir."

The house was still. Or some would have described it that way. Actually the night was full of sound. There was the occasional grumble of distant thunder and the steady drubbing of rain against windows. The gutters gurgled. Nell, in her bathrobe, made her way to the front of the little house and peered out through the dining room window at the streetlamp. Rain slanted through its cone of light and the pavement shone. A good night to be tucked up inside, she told herself.

She decided to treat herself to a tot.

"Drinking alone now," she continued. "And talking to yourself too! Get a grip, madam. Next you'll be thinking fondly about Lloyd."

Holding a rocks glass of sherry, she wandered back through the house to the window that held the view of the backyard and her neighbor Bunty Whitney's studio, dark now. And then, as if summoned, into the room came the rare ghost of Lloyd Bane.

Nell was never sure what to call Lloyd. Ex-husband? Late husband? Their marriage had been long and labored. It was not a noisy marriage or even an argumentative one. Rather, it was a dull legal arrangement between two dissimilar people who gradually grew farther and farther apart. Someone had attempted once to explain logarithmic progression to Nell. Who was that? Oh, yes. Franklin Fitzmaurice, and they'd been at a party somewhere. Franklin had been holding forth to a baffled Nell and finally, frustrated with her obtuseness, had taken a pen and a folded piece of paper from a breast pocket.

"Here," he'd said, placing the paper on the top of the host's grand piano and making two marks close together, "two squibs. See how close they are at the start?"

Nell, peering, had nodded dubiously.

"Okay, but each has a slightly different orientation—just two degrees of difference. That isn't much, is it? But as you extend each line out over time," instructed Franklin, drawing with his bloody fountain pen, "the separation widens. The distance between the lines increases until here—out here—you have a wide gulf. A chasm."

Nell had viewed the diagram over Franklin's gray tweed arm and seen his point and in a clap of insight had understood that here was a diagram of her relationship with Lloyd Bane.

Eventually the discomfort of trying a share a life with someone so different had galvanized Nell to action. She'd asked Lloyd for a separation and then for a divorce. It had been a long process—and an expensive one—but Nell bought her freedom. She had come out feeling like she was emerging from a long, dark tunnel into daylight. And fresh air! She'd drawn in great breaths of it.

Then Lloyd had died suddenly. On a treadmill apparently. In a gym. This amazed Nell for Lloyd had been a famously sedentary man, but evidently he'd been turning over a new leaf. Perhaps had signed up for a dating service as well as taken a gym membership. Nell had tried to muster up sorrow at Lloyd's passing and had even managed some, but on balance she'd been surprised at how little emotion she actually did feel.

She sipped the sherry, wondering if the memories the Etons were dredging up were responsible for this plunge into her own past.

"Enough!" she declared. "Time to return to the present."

She set the sherry glass down with a smart smack on the marble counter. She was going to take the drafts of *The War Years* to Tice and Bella in the morning and would soon begin the third-quarter of the double memoir. *The Bountiful Years*, it would be called.

Chapter 15

Tice Eton was parked, as usual, by the front windows and appeared to be gazing over the Common. Or perhaps he was gazing at nothing but his thoughts. Nell couldn't be sure. For a moment she was struck by his age and he wore an invisible mantle of vulnerability like a shawl. She shivered and pledged to herself to accelerate work on his memoir. But then Tice, feeling her presence, turned with a welcoming smile.

"Nell," he said with pleasure. "My dear. Come in and tell me your stories and I shall tell you mine."

The impression of fragility burst like a soap bubble and Nell, smiling also, stepped toward his wheelchair.

"We are entering a new phase," she told him. "We're halfway through the process now and you and Bella are going to talk about the years after the war. They were good years for you, I think. Years when you started your family and built up your business."

"Yes, good years they were on balance," Tice said. "But when I got back from Europe, all was not well."

Excerpt from
The Bountiful Years
Prentice Eton

I came up to Boston from New York by train after my ship docked, and the whole way I thought of little else than marrying Arabella Whiteside. But when I got to Salem—to this very house on North Federal Square—I found that my father was terribly frail. I knew he had been ill all summer, but I wasn't prepared for how weak he'd become. And I'm not sure he knew me. That was hard. My mother sat by his bed and spoke to him in a loud, flat voice. "Tice is here now, dearest. Our boy is home safe. Can you say hello to Tice, George?"

And when he turned his face toward me, I saw his skin was practically transparent. Waxen. And I could see the blue veins in his temples and I thought how his blood was pulsing slowly, very slowly, through his body. My own body went cold with dread and I felt a weight bearing down on me that was different from anything I'd ever experienced.

But there was nothing to do but go on, and so Bella and I made plans to marry right after Christmas. Because of everything—my father's illness, my war wounds, even the war itself that was still pressing on everything around us, the ceremony was very simple. Intimate my new mother-in-law called it. Well, she was trying to make the best of things and I loved her for it. The Whitesides' Congregational minister performed the ceremony in the family's sitting room on Pinckney Street, and Bella and I had a honeymoon in Montreal. All of four days, it was, including the daylong train rides there and back.

My father passed away three weeks later.

Bella and I had planned to rent a starter apartment in Boston so I could be near the office. I was taking my father's place in Eton, Jennings and Cogswell, but the plan collapsed when my father died. Mother couldn't be expected to keep this house alone so Bella and I set up housekeeping here.

Mother tried to be sensitive. She moved into an apartment on the third floor to give the newlyweds space and some sense of our own place. But sadly, she went rapidly downhill and within a few months joined my father in the Eton plot.

Bella and I lost no time in establishing our own little family.

Caroline, named for my sister, was born before 1945 ended and before Christmas the following year, her baby brother George was kicking in his bassinet. George. My son. My assurance that the Eton name would see its way into a new generation. Funny, isn't it, to hold a newborn infant and see in him the man he will become and the children he will sire.

Eton, Jennings and Cogswell is a private investment firm and during the war years, my father and his partners managed it with great perspicacity. I think I'm not being too modest in saying that the firm continued thrive in the years after the war when I occupied my late father's corner office. Phillip Jennings and Alastair Cogswell moved along into retirement and several very sharp young men joined the firm and were eventually made partners. Those years were busy: long hours in the office for me, and for Bella, long hours as the mother of small children who required a good deal of attention.

Bella wanted Caroline and George to have the summer experiences she and her sisters had enjoyed, so they spent their summers at Squam, sharing Eastwind with Sybil and Martha and ultimately with their offspring. As Bella's father had, I came up by train some weekends and joined them for the month of August.

Even before the war started, The Rocks had been sold. I thought sometimes of taking the children to Goose Rocks to show them where their pa had spent his boyhood. I could see myself walking along the beach, especially with George, but then a shade would pass over me and I couldn't do it. I had the weird superstition that if I took George to Goose Rocks—if he were to walk with me in the places where I'd walked with Willard—then something terrible—something unspeakable—would happen to the little fellow. And so I...well, I just didn't go.

#

In those years when life was sweet and busy, Bella and I began to find great satisfaction in charitable enterprises as both sets of our parents had done. We enjoyed music and had season tickets for years at the Boston Symphony. In summers we'd occasionally journey to Tanglewood to picnic on the lawn and listen to the Boston Pops rehearsals. The Peabody Essex Museum—our little backwater museum here in Salem—wasn't much of a cultural treasure in those days but Bella and I had an idea of what it could become. Not necessarily of all it ultimately did become—which is grander than we dreamt possible—but we supported it as generously as we could with money and time.

And South Union church, of course, absorbed much of our time and interest. I served as moderator on three separate occasions and was on the Diaconate. We saw five different ministers in the South Union pulpit over our years, and I served on two search committees and Bella served on one. And when it was time for an ambitious capital fund raising campaign, I was told that I was the individual who could be most effective. I hope that was true. I think it might have been because the campaign raised over a million dollars.

Bella had her own charitable interests, and thanks to trusts set up by her family, she was able to make significant monetary contributions, but she was also generous with her time.

Fruitful years they were. Bountiful years—is that what we're calling this period? And they were very good years. God was good to us and I think we were able to share that grace so generously given.

Chapter 16

As usual, Bella Eton led Nell to the sunroom.

"Ready to talk about the bountiful years?" Nell asked.

"Is that what we're calling them? Well, they were! And the memories are pleasant. I will enjoy this."

Bella seated herself in her customary armchair, folded her hands in her lap and regarded Nell brightly. She looked, Nell decided, like a schoolchild anticipating a recitation for which she was well prepared—keen to display her preparation.

Today Bella was wearing a grey wool skirt and a cashmere twinset in a grey that was several shades lighter. The affect set off her clear-white hair to good advantage.

"Well then," Nell coached. "Let's begin."

Excerpt from
The Bountiful Years
Arabella Whiteside Eton

The war ended for Tice just before Christmas, and I suppose it ended then for me as well. Home he came and I could hardly take my eyes off him. Remember, except for a couple of short leaves he'd had in 1941 before he went overseas, it had been four years since I'd seen him. I couldn't believe it was really Tice. He was much thinner and he looked very distinguished, I thought, in his uniform. And he wanted to get married right away.

When we'd talked of marriage before the war, my idea of our wedding featured a long church aisle and eight bridesmaids treading down it one by one and then, to the strains of Mendelssohn's Wedding March, down I'd come, floating on my father's arm. But it didn't happen that way. Tice's father was very ill, and what with one consideration and another, practicality ruled the day. We were married very simply in my parents' sitting room. And instead of a white gown, I wore a simple dress. Cornflower blue, my favorite color, and my youngest sister Martha served as my maid of honor and single bridesmaid. My sister Sybil had joined the Women's Army Corps and couldn't get home from Washington D.C. where she was stationed.

Our first home didn't work out the way we'd envisioned either. When Tice's father died, we moved into the house in Salem. Mother Eton was very sensitive. She gathered herself and her most precious things into an apartment on the third floor and more or less gave us the house to manage as we liked.

I hadn't expected to live in Salem—at least not right away. The town and the people in it were unfamiliar and I felt disoriented and even a bit lonely. But almost immediately I found I was expecting a baby. I know Tice was hoping for a son, for he was very keen on founding a little dynasty to carry on the Eton name. After Willard died, I think Tice felt it all depended upon him to carry on the family name and that lent a curious sort of pressure. But I was secretly pleased to have a daughter, and I welcomed Caroline with all my heart. And eleven months later, Tice got his wish. A son. Our son George. And then, for some reason, no more babies came. And so the perpetuation of the Eton name ultimately fell to George.

As the children grew and developed interests of their own, I was able to more fully develop mine. Tice and I were both very keen to see the local museum—the Peabody Essex Museum—evolve to its potential, and we were active quite early in this cause, although it took years before the pokey little museum grew into the magnificent Moshe Safdie-designed structure that it is today. Oh, there were a number of artistic and humanitarian causes that Tice and I supported with our time, interest and money, but there were some causes in which we participated individually. One that was—and still is—dear to my heart is Planned Parenthood. When I began lending support, the year was 1947 and contraception was still illegal in Massachusetts. The few clinics that had been established in the state in the early 'thirties had all been closed down and shuttered by 1938. It was considered somewhat radical—even scandalous by some—to advocate for contraception, and it wasn't a very popular or correct decision to support PPL to the extent I did. I don't think Tice entirely approved, but he had the grace—and the good sense, if truth be known—not to make an issue of it.

"My wife, the activist," he used to say, tongue-in-cheek.

Well, contraception was outside the law of the Commonwealth in those days. In 1940 there was a poll that showed that eighty-two percent of Massachusetts citizens favored contraception—most didn't understand that it was illegal in the Commonwealth—and there was even a referendum on the ballot that would permit married persons to practice birth control. Imagine that! Those old legislators in the State House trying to govern what when on in peoples' bedrooms! And the stupid old things mustered a fifty-eight percent majority to defeat the referendum. So it went down in defeat and physicians weren't permitted to prescribe birth control until 1966!

I was also an advocate for HAWK—an agency based right in Salem that works against domestic abuse of all kinds. It does wonderful work and I've been privileged to support it and join in the efforts to work for change.

It is very satisfying to use one's resources in support of causes that work against abuse and for a woman's reproductive rights.

Oh, but the years have been good to us. Tice and I had our health, our children grew and flourished, and we had dear, dear friends around us. Arthur and Emily Hutchins...Ted and Mildred Lord... we've been so blessed, Tice and I. We have been so happy.

Chapter 17

"You're no any fun anymore," Bunty Whitney observed. "You've been beavering away on that Eton project with scarcely time to come up for air. Can't you take a break?"

"Time is not our friend with this book," Nell admitted. "The Etons are quite anxious to see it finished and placed into the hands of their heirs. They call them the Grands and the Greats, by the way. And they've developed a plan to summon the Greats to Salem for visits as soon as the book is finished. These kids are going to meet their great-grandparents for the first time and each will receive—presumably with great ceremony—a copy of the memoir. And they'll each get a face-full of family, if I'm any judge."

"So they're in a hurry, the Etons. Are they fearful that one of them will be nipped off the stem before the book is finished?"

"Hmmm. *Time that blows on the kettle's rim, waits to carry us off,* Nell murmured reflectively.

"That's pretty good," Bunty said. "Did you just make that up?"

76

"No, Maxine Kumin did. But the thing is, I don't want to be the one to delay the project."

Besides," pointed out the ever-practical Bunty. "You don't get the final payment until the book is delivered."

Nell grinned. "Okay, then, what'll we get up to?"

"Road trip." Bunty was decisive. "Peterborough, New Hampshire. Poke through the artsy shops in Depot Square and have lunch at the good old-fashioned Peterborough Diner."

"Why stop there?" Nell said. "Let's do a whole diner experience. There's Moody's Diner in Waldoboro Maine. . . ."

"And don't forget our own Agawam Diner right down the road," Bunty put in. "Coconut cream pie—yum-yum."

"And I can be on the prowl for new soup recipes," Nell said. "Okay, Ms. Whitney, grab your coat and get your hat; prepare to leave all worries on the doorstep."

CORN CHOWDER
(With a nod toward Moody's Diner)
4 slices of thick bacon, diced
1/2 cup chopped onion
2 cups diced potatoes
2 cups boiling water
2 Tbl. butter
1 tsp kosher salt
1 10-oz can of creamed corn
1 12-oz can of evaporated milk

Brown the bacon until crisp and remove from the skillet. Wipe out the skillet and sauté the onion in the butter. Add the water, potatoes and salt and simmer until the potatoes are tender. Add the creamed corn and evaporated milk. Let the chowder sit for 30 minutes before serving so the flavors blend.

Chapter 18

"Vintage years. That's just a flossy way of saying old age, isn't it?"

Prentice Eton had peered provocatively over his eyeglasses at Nell as he said this, and she had to grin. He'd had her stymied for a few seconds though, and uncharacteristically, she hadn't come up with a witty retort.

"Look at it this way," she'd said persuasively, "this is the last quarter of the Eton memoir. The home stretch. The time has come to sum up the past and bless the present and future."

Tice had given her a long, evaluating look before finally smiling decisively.

"Point taken. I think I'll choose to accept that position," he had said. "I never thought I would get to this place in my life, but now I'm here. Bring it on!"

"But this is your story," Nell told him. "I'm the one to say bring it on."

"Very well then," the old man said. He seemed to be considering. "Let's do the wrap-up."

Excerpt from
The Vintage Years
Prentice Eton

I guess I didn't feel old until George died. Bella and I had lost our daughter Caroline seven months earlier—and that was a tremendous blow—but the news of George's death coming so soon after that first shock, knocked the breath right out of me. A son. The loss of a son. He'd been meant to carry on the family name, and he had done that of course—he and Barbara had produced Michael. But Michael was still a small boy. The little fellow was living on the other side of the continent, and he was going to finish growing up without a father to guide him. He would never have that direct connection to his Eton kin back on the East Coast.

A parent isn't supposed to outlive a child—even a grown child. For me the old order was shaken and shaken badly. Suddenly I was ten-years-old again and my brother Willard was gone. Gone in the wash of a single rogue wave. I felt worse than I had that dreadful summer in Maine—full of grief and anger. Fruitless anger for there was no sensible target for it. If I could have gotten an axe and destroyed something the way I'd hacked into the hull of *Goosie,* I would have done so. But as a grown man, there was nothing to do but slip an arm around Arabella—poor grieving Bella—and stand tall. I had to carry on as my father had.

But that's when I realized for the first time that I was old. Vulnerable and, well—old.

# # #

I felt vulnerable again when I had the stroke. The episode itself wasn't really that terrible to experience: one moment I was sitting at my desk in the study upstairs and the next thing I knew, I was in a hospital bed looking up at Bella's worried face.

Then there was the convalescence—a very nice therapist named Judy came every day for several weeks to help me. And Frank Largent, upon whom we'd always depended to keep the house in good order, took on the other very significant job of caregiver. I'd become an old man. All of Judy's good work couldn't put my pins back under me, and I had to accept the wheelchair and learn to be grateful that my mental faculties were intact. I could still use my hands and arms, so thankfully I could continue to do a little work, feed myself and so forth. But Frank became my constant companion, helping me with the most intimate and personal things—at this point, closer to me even than Bella.

I had a choice then. I could refuse to accept what life had delivered or I could refuse to let fate's hand deliver a crippling blow to my attitude as well as my body. The latter was my choice. I refused to give in to self-pity.

But the stroke was a wake-up call. I made sure our house was in order. I finally turned the reins of Eton, Jennings and Cogswell over to my younger partners. I wasn't going to the office full time at that point, but I'd continued to keep my nose in the game. Clearly it was time to take my nose all the way out. I imagine the partners were relieved.

Bella and I called in our attorney, John Dockery, and reviewed our trusts and wills and made certain that our bequests were as we wanted them. Bella was well-provided for, of course, but I was concerned for the grief she would face when I was gone. Finally, she and I sat with Benjamin Wallace, our minister, and laid out the plans for my memorial service. All will be ready when I am finally ready to leave this life.

# # #

Now since we are calling these the vintage years, I want to point out that vintage suggests abundance, and so I don't intend to end this memoir on a discouraging note. I'll leave this earth of sound mind and of good cheer. I will leave recognizing and celebrating God's goodness. Yes, there have been losses—some terrible ones—but these have been more than balanced by gifts of grace. I grew up knowing the support and protection of a loving family. My parents and grandparents provided a life of consistency and financial stability that laid a sound foundation for manhood. I participated in a great war. I was part of what would be later called the greatest generation. I don't know whether that's true, but I'd like to think it is. And I came out of that war alive and whole. Many didn't. I came home. And I came home to Bella. My beautiful wife. We've lived together and loved each other for sixty years. We had two children together.

Family resources and our own hard work have ensured we never had to worry about the exigencies of life. Every material thing we needed was there for us, and we've been able to share our bounty through various philanthropies in the hope that artistic endeavors, human decency and the established social order will be perpetuated.

Finally, through our grandchildren and through our great-grandchildren, Arabella and I are able to see a new generation growing up and becoming ready to take on the responsibilities of being an Eton. We trust to them much. And we hold the confidence that they will honor the family legacy and the name of Eton.

Chapter 19

"I think I'll be a bit sad to see these sessions end," Arabella said. And indeed she did look a bit down.

"But just think," Nell said, "you'll soon have your book, finished, proofed and professionally packaged with a smart, shiny, four-color cover. We'll have to talk about that cover, by the way. This next step, Bella, can be the most fun. The baby is about to be born. We're just starting the last great creative push!"

Arabella Eton laughed.

"What I will miss—and don't try to talk me out of it, young lady—is seeing you regularly. Anticipating your visits has been so good for me and for Tice. And you've provided an amazing therapy through this business of looking backward with its challenge of trying to remember things—oh, the little details—of our lives. It has been excellent for Tice, and I'm so thankful to see how well he has reacted to the memoir process."

"Then let's move along," Nell said. "What are the vintage years like for Arabella Eton?"

Excerpt from
The Vintage Years
Arabella Whiteside Eton

Where do the vintage years begin? Where did the bountiful years end? I'm not sure I can know, but this I do know ...

Our children grew up and found people whom they believed they would love throughout their lifetimes the way Tice and I loved each other. The way we lived with each other. That's what they seemed to want anyway, and perhaps it's what they thought they'd found. But Tice and I had our reservations.

Caroline was first. She was barely twenty when she brought Elison Danbridge into this house. Right into this room! And she said, "Mama, Papa, Eli and I want to get married and if you say no, we'll go right ahead and marry anyway."

We were speechless. Even Tice couldn't manage a single word. Caroline had never talked that way to us, but she stood right there with her chin up in the air and a chip on her shoulder and dared us to say no. Well, we talked and talked to them. Not trying to dissuade them exactly but trying to get them to buy some time.

Elison Danbridge stayed the weekend as our guest, and we got to know a bit about him but by Monday morning, Tice and I were no happier about the marriage. And the young people were just as pig-headed about it as when they'd arrived with the news.

So Caroline and Eli were married right here in this house just three weeks later. And I felt cheated of a second white church wedding. Caroline wore a summer dress—a halter dress—splashed with loud flowers. A dress she'd worn dozens of times to picnics and pubs and wherever. It was as though she didn't want to make the occasion anything special. Tice finally prevailed upon Eli to wear a necktie. And the young man eventually consented, but he left the knot askew and hanging a good inch below the collar button. He was a consummate passive aggressive personality.

They moved immediately to Minnesota where Eli supposedly had some sort of job waiting. Six months later we learned in a letter that Caroline was pregnant. I went out to St Paul when Martha was born, and it was already plain that Caroline and Eli weren't happy together. I wanted Caroline to come home—home to Salem—and bring the baby, but she refused, and four years later, the marriage collapsed for good. Either she walked out or Eli did, we never knew, and now it doesn't matter who did what, but it was over and our hearts ached for our daughter's unhappiness. And instead of returning to Salem, Caroline marched off to Florida—to Ponte Vedra—and raised little Martha there.

#

We had higher hopes for George. He and Barbara were engaged for three years and it dragged on until we thought they'd never marry! But of course they did and when they had Michael, Tice was over the moon. The Eton name would continue he felt. The only drawback was George and Barbara were living on the West Coast and George was traveling a lot for business. We made several trips to the Coast to visit, but I think George only brought his family East once. And we hardly knew little Michael.

And then came that terrible year—the year Caroline died of that horrid melanoma and poor George dropped dead seven months later. Barbara remarried almost immediately and Michael was withdrawn from us even further. And life, which had been so good to us, seemed to have taken a sour turn indeed.

#

Oh, we carried on, Tice and I. Life wasn't all dismal. We were still active in the charities and interests we'd developed along the way. And we had wonderful friends, although even here, there was loss. One by one our dear friends dropped away and sometimes it seemed that funerals and wakes were our heaviest social commitments. Funerals and doctors' visits. And then Tice suffered that stroke. I was sick with worry, but he was magnificent. He recovered so well, except for his legs, of course. But he is as bright and sharp as he ever was. Frank Largent became Tice's caregiver and there, as well, we are fortunate. And we're fortunate in Henny too. Henny DeFelice has been housekeeper and dear friend for so long. She is marvelous company for me every day.

#

I think every person needs a reason to get up in the morning. Everyone needs things to look forward to. Simple things. Reasons that make life worth living. Perhaps in the vintage years that becomes more important than ever, even though the things one looks forward too may seem far less exciting. There are no Super Bowl tickets...no trips to Paris and Rome...no longer any cruises to Alaska or the Panama Canal. But there are amazing reasons to open your eyes every morning. Things like the returning birds in spring, the clematis that has bloomed for thirty years on the lamppost and the fact that your husband of more than sixty years is sitting across from you at the breakfast table. And not only is he sitting there, but he is smiling and sharing his opinions of the political race and the new museum director and wondering whether the church sexton has a bottle of whiskey stashed in the broom closet. Neither of you needs to hurry off to an office or a meeting or an appointment. You are free, if you choose, to pour a second cup of coffee or even a third and continue to sit as the sunshine pours onto the breakfast table. The toast is crisp, made from Henny's homemade Portuguese bread, and the jam in the pot is last summer's blueberry jam and it tastes just right. You don't take all this for granted, that's the thing, when you're in your vintage years. You don't take any of it for granted. Rather you see it as a gift of grace. I always think of Robert Browning's *Pippa's Song—God's in His heaven—All's right with the world!*

In the vintage years, one is so grateful.

Chapter 20

Robert Hutchins had come to Salem to join the Etons for Nell's presentation. She had pronounced the final draft of the double memoir complete and now stood with three bound copies, ready to place them in the hands of Robert, Prentice and Arabella

"Before I give you these," she said, "I want to say a few words about the title I've chosen. You are, of course, completely free to disagree with it and to come up with a title you like better. Also you will each want to read the final drafts carefully. You've seen the work at stages all through the writing process, but this will be the first time you see the entire manuscript. I expect any comments to be minor, but please do indicate any changes you'd like to see."

Nell sensed anticipation from her three listeners. Bella was sitting on the edge of her seat—vey straight—and Tice was leaning forward in his wheelchair. She smiled.

"Now the title. I am proposing to call this book *Looking Forward: The Memoirs of Prentice and Arabella Eton.*"

Nell paused, but only long enough to look each listener in the eye. Then she continued.

"There is a slight irony here since a memoir suggests, by its very name, a retrospective. By declaring that this memoir looks forward, however, your book foreshadows your unique interest in the future—both the futures of your great-grandchildren and their offspring as well as the futures of the social and cultural issues and institutions that you support and in which you believe. The philanthropic activities that have distinguished your lives."

Nell paused again, waiting for the others to absorb her idea.

"Furthermore," she continued, "I think there should be a foreword that explains this concept and I am proposing Robert as the author of this forward. I will ghostwrite it, if you'd prefer not to write it yourself, Robert. In fact, I've started a draft. I would like to read this to you and see what you think."

Tice cleared his throat.

"By all means, my dear. You have our complete attention. Please go ahead."

And so Nell did.

A memoir is by definition a backward look. A trip into memory that calls up experiences and images that are shadowed in the past and puts them on view in the present—in the pages of a book. This particular book is unusual for several reasons. For one, it is a double memoir. In it, the memories of a long-married couple, Prentice and Arabella Eton, are twined.

The title, as titles should, hints at the content. This memoir looks forward because Prentice and Arabella Eton have looked forward all their lives They have lived their lives with concern for those who will come after them. And while these individuals certainly include subsequent generations of Etons, the concern doesn't stop with family. The Etons' philanthropies extend into the arts and areas of social concern. Prentice and Arabella Eton have always held a vision for a brighter, more perfect future and have worked to accomplish that goal.

In creating the memoir, they continue to look forward, and they dedicate this book to their great-grandchildren, through whom future generations of Etons will continue.

I have known (and loved) Prentice and Arabella all my life. They were dear friends of my late parents who, I believe, introduced them to each other. Prentice and Arabella are like family to me and I am proud of their many achievements— one of which is this splendid memoir. ..... Robert C. Hutchins

Silence followed this reading and as Nell closed the manuscript, Robert Hutchins cleared his throat.

"I should be very proud to attach my name to the foreword," he said. "And I don't think I could improve at all on these words, Nell."

He looked questioningly at the others, seeking validation, which Prentice and Arabella were swift to supply. Suddenly everyone was talking at once, agreeing that the book's title was exactly right and imagining the pleasure and surprise the Greats would express when receiving their inscribed copies.

Offstage at last, Nell smiled as she leaned back in her chair and listened to the happy babble around her. At last.

Chapter 21

Jerry Gasso was cooking. Nell and Robert Hutchins were watching him.

"He gets these spasms," Robert explained to Nell, "and starts preparing these elaborate meals. Trouble is, Jerry likes an audience while he cooks and the bigger the audience, the better."

"Yes, the show is full swing," Jerry said, brandishing a chef's knife and sounding a little peevish. "So where is Madeline? She's missing the chopping. It's one of the best parts of the preparation!"

"She'll be here," Nell said soothingly. "It takes a few minutes to walk over from Bay Village, you know."

Robert edged behind Jerry, reached the refrigerator and extracted a bottle of prosecco. He waved it at Jerry, who shook his head.

"The cook is drinking beer," said the cook, and demonstrated by taking a long pull on a bottle Anchor Steam. Robert poured the prosecco's pale, vibrant bubbles of into two flutes and added St. Germaine.

Nell raised her glass.

"Let's drink to the Etons' enthusiastic acceptance of the memoir's final draft," she said. "I feel like celebrating tonight."

"Congratulations," Robert told her. "I know they are pleased. More than pleased. Delighted with the draft and they can't wait to have their book in their hands."

"And so you're taking it on from here," Nell prompted.

"Yep. I've handed it off to the proofreaders and then it will go to the designers for layout and cover art and as soon as those steps are complete, we'll upload the text and cover, get a couple of proof copies, and the whole kit-and-caboodle will be ready. I love the title by the way."

"What is it again?" Jerry asked. He didn't lift his eyes from the chopping board.

"*Looking Forward*," Nell told him.

Jerry raised his eyes looking puzzled.

"Looking backward, don't you mean? It is a memoir."

"No, forward," Nell insisted. "Remember, these are philanthropists. Tice and Bella care deeply about preserving the very best for the future—that is, for the generations of their own family who are still to come. They hope to perpetuate the values they regard as civilized and socially responsible."

"Huh," said Jerry. He picked up a carrot.

"Can I do anything to help?" Nell asked.

"Cooking, no, but you could check the table. See if everything looks okay."

Nell did so. The dining room in the Beacon Hill townhouse was long and narrow, so Jerry had visually enlarged it with a wall of mirrors on one of the narrow ends and a banquette under the windows on the street side. This bought space for the long table and the fleet of chairs on the table's opposite side. There were two centerpieces and chargers under the dinner plates. There were salad plates on the dinner plates, and linen napkins, pick-stitched and monogramed, were placed with a studied casualness beside the forks. The room looked delectable and Nell was envious. And there was nothing she could add to improve the presentation.

The doorbell rang and Robert, with the flourish of a magician displaying the lady who has not, after all, been sawed in half, appeared from the foyer with Madeline Kaiser. Nell, as always, was delighted to see her elfish friend—tiny as Puck and nearly as mischievous.

"My God!" shouted Jerry when they trooped into the kitchen. "She's finally here! We'd given up all hope. Well, you missed the massacre of the vegetables, Madeline. I'm sorry but I couldn't delay their *coup de grace* any longer."

But by way of excusing her lateness, Madeline supplied a story about her walk to the Hill.

"So this man stops me," she explained. "Right by that ghastly horse statue on the Common. Very odd-looking fellow. He's wearing a bathrobe over his business suit. Brocade. Silk lapels. Oh, and bedroom slippers—blue corduroy things. Anyhow, he asks me if I'd mind answering a question. So what the hell, I say no, I wouldn't mind."

Madeline Kaiser had a flair for drama, and she paused in her narration for affect. Her eyes sparkled wickedly.

"He says—and can you believe this?—he says, if someone were going to drive a tank over your feet, what color shoes would you like to be wearing? Isn't that bizarre?"

She giggled.

"What d'you suppose he was thinking?"

"He was a foot fetishist, darling," Jerry Gasso told her. "But what was your answer? Or did you just turn and run?"

"No," cried Madeline, "I told him black patent-leather Mary-Janes!"

And she and Jerry burst out laughing. Nell laughed too, shaking her head.

"Don't you know better than to talk to strangers, Madeline?"

Madeline Kaiser looked at Nell with eyebrows arched innocently.

"But that way you miss out on so much fun!"

"Speaking of fun, we're drinking prosecco with St. Germaine, Madeline," Robert Hutchins told her. "Some for you? But you could have scotch, or even one of Jerry's beers. We're celebrating the final draft, and the acceptance thereof, of the Etons' memoirs"

"Ooh, congratulations indeed, Nell. And yes, Robert, prosecco and St. Germaine will be perfect."

"Drink up! Drink up!" Jerry chimed. "This entire casserole is on its way to the oven and I am about to plate the salads. I promise you, friends and neighbors, this is going to be a fantastic meal."

Chapter 22

On an evening in early spring, Nell and Bunty Whitney made their way over the brick sidewalk toward the Etons' house on North Federal Square. Bunty, Nell could see, had made an effort to dress for the occasion. She had twisted her hair so ruthlessly and jabbed it so full of tortoise shell pins that it wouldn't dare to come undone and fly all about in its usual disarray. And from the hinterlands of her closet she had produced a brocade caftan with all the colors of the crown jewels. Nell appreciated her efforts and thought Bunty looked very nice.

"Ouch!" Bunty complained. "I'm not used to these cutie shoes! It'll be a miracle if I don't sprain an ankle sliding off one of these damn bricks!"

Nell smiled.

"Almost there," she said, "and I must say Bunty, you do look splendid."

"Well, I tried," Bunty said. "I know this book signing party is important to you, and it will be riddled with important people—people in the arts—and I am quite gratified to be coming as your guest."

"You'll fit in like a greased hand slides into a silk glove. Now here we are."

And Nell took Bunty's elbow and steered her up the granite steps of the Eton house.

The door opened immediately and Frank Largent loomed in the doorway. His moon-face beamed above a scarlet bow tie.

"Henny and Bella are running their tootsies off," he said, "so I'm doing door duty as well as tending bar. A handy arrangement because I can greet the guests and get their drink orders in one fell swoop. So good evening and what'll you have?"

Nell was delighted.

"You look marvelous, Frank. Stupendous tie, by the way. And this is my friend Bunty Whitney."

Bunty thrust out her hand.

"Very pleased to meet you and a whiskey and soda would be perfect."

"White wine, please Frank. Coats in the library?"

Henny DeFelice sailed past with a tray of bacon-wrapped chicken livers and a wave. She literally sparkled with excitement and bling.

The house was already filled with people and the noise of a good party. Through the living room's wide, arched door, Nell saw Robert Hutchins raise a long arm and wave. She guided Bunty into the throng, turning her hips sideways and crab-walking to get to the window where Robert stood with Jerry Gasso and a couple Nell did not know. Robert introduced them. The couple turned out to have some connection with the Peabody Essex Museum and Bunty immediately asked a provocative question that launched a lively discussion.

Robert drew Nell slightly aside.

"Tice is planning to make a speech but I'm to make the introduction. Don't stray too far from the fireplace. That's going to be the stage."

He winked at her.

"Oh dear," said Nell. "I was hoping to blend into the wallpaper. I won't have to say anything, will I?"

But Robert Hutchins, obeying some invisible signal, was suddenly making his way toward the fireplace where Tice's wheelchair was already parked. Bella materialized, apparently summoned also, and Henny hurried after her, reaching to untie the frilly little apron Bella wore.

"It won't do," Henny hissed, "to stand there looking like a hausfrau in your moment of glory!"

Robert clapped his hands.

"May I have your attention, please. Attention?" From the window, Jerry Gasso released a shrill whistle, then looked around in mock who-did-that innocence. But the party noise subsided quickly and guests shifted, each to gain a better view of the proceedings shaping up by the fireplace.

"This is a very special occasion for my dear friends Bella and Tice Eton," Robert said. "In their long lifetimes of many wonderful events, this is a first. Tonight they have invited you here to celebrate the publication of their memoir."

Robert held up a copy of the book.

"Ladies and gentlemen, may I present *Looking Forward: The Memoirs of Prentice and Arabella Eton*. And now it is my good pleasure to present the new authors—Tice and Bella."

Applause and some genteel cheers greeted this speech, but these were quickly hushed when Tice Eton, grinning like a young man who has just hit a home run or scored a winning touchdown, began to speak.

"For Bella and me, this evening is the culmination of a long season of work and a wish that we held for a dozen years or more. We wanted—we yearned—to have a book that gave a good and full account of our lives. Our lives together as a loving couple but beyond that, a chronicle of the families who shaped us. In short, we wanted a memoir. We wanted our grandchildren and especially our great-grandchildren to understand their family connections and to better know themselves through knowing their ancestors."

Tice paused and reached for Bella's hand.

"Well, now we have our memoir—thanks to two special people. The first is Robert Hutchins, whom we have known all his life. He is the child, you see, of Arthur and Emily Hutchins—dear friends who introduced Bella and me when we were young. Dear friends who are with us still, but only in memory. But Robert is here and he is like a son to us. And when we asked him to help us find the right person to assist with our memoir, he said there was only one person whom we should consider. As usual, Robert was quite right. And here is that one person: dear friends, may I present to you Nell Bane."

Jerry Gasso seized Nell's hand and people parted to let him lead her to the fireplace. Nell nodded shyly in acknowledgement of the polite applause.

"Every minute of this project," she told them, "was a joy. Everyone here knows Tice and Bella, so you know how fascinating and gracious they are. I think some of you might envy me the time I've been allowed to spend with them and the stories I've been privy to. They were perfect clients. And if they are pleased with their memoir, I am very gratified."

Nell looked pleadingly at Robert who patted her shoulder and obligingly stepped forward to take the floor away from her.

"Now Bella, my dear," Tice continued, and on cue Bella stepped forward with two books which she ceremoniously presented to Robert and Nell.

Tice again addressed his guests. "There is a book for each of you as well," he told them, "and if you wish to have them autographed, Bella and I will be very happy to sign the books for you. Mind you, the signatures may reduce the value somewhat, but the decision is yours."

He chuckled.

Frank Largent rolled out a drinks cart that had been stacked with copies of *Looking Forward* and people began eagerly helping themselves to books and instantly thumbing through them.

Nell escaped back to the window where Bunty still stood with her new PEM friends.

"Well done," Bunty told her. "A nice little speech. Your voice was clear and could be heard all around the room. And you didn't fall down or throw up. I was proud of you."

Now, with the presentation successfully over, Nell began to enjoy the party. Guests revolved past, asking questions, complementing her and two people even insisted that Nell Bane add her signature to the flyleaves of their books right under the autographs of Prentice and Arabella Eton.

But Tice Eton was still excited. He took the floor once again.

"But there is more to come," he announced. "And now," he confided to his guests, "now Bella and I are looking forward to the next phase of our plan. We have invited our three great-grandchildren to visit—one at a time—so each can get to know us and can better know their family through conversations and through the memoir. Each will receive copies of the memoir along with special, handwritten notes from their doddering old great-grandparents. We hope their visits will enable them to create memories of their own—memories that will be lifelong. But now, kind friends all, thank you for coming out tonight to make this event all the more special for Bella and me. I drink to all of you—to your good health and good humor."

And the old man lifted his glass high and held it steady there, in the air, while the roomful of people hurried to raise glasses too and to echo the words of his toast.

Chapter 23

Nell was in the chips. That's how she thought of it. All the lovely bucks from the Etons' memoir project were rolling around in her bank account, building up interest through the magic of compounding. Nell had never been terribly clear just how that worked but it was a darling concept. Moreover, after weeks of working right straight out to produce that double memoir, Nell's time was now her own. No other ghostwriting projects were quivering on the horizon, although the continuing commitment to Tice and Bella was shimmering just below the horizon, for the first one of the Greats was arriving shortly. Brittany, the eldest great-grandchild, would be traveling from Chicago where she had a job in marketing, and Nell had offered to show her the New England coast. So the ghostwriter was turning docent and the chips, therefore, would keep rolling in.

"I'm in the chips, Madeline," she told her friend. "How'd you like to see that new play at the Wilbur and have lunch somewhere on Newbury Street? My treat."

Madeline Kaiser declared that she would like that very much.

And as long as she'd gone all the way to Boston, Nell decided it was a shame to waste the trip, so she stopped into Linens on the Hill where she stood herself to a handsome set of French linen sheets.

Then word came that Brittany Baker had arrived from Chicago. The first great-grandchild had politely declined offers to be picked up at Logan and instead, had rented an economy car at the airport and made her way to Salem with guidance from a GPS.

Nell was impressed. But she knew her own days of leisure were about to end, so in a single last splash-out, she drove over to Tannery Marketplace where she spent a mood-altering half hour in The Red Bird Trading Company fingering upholstery swatches and long sweaters made of materials that exceeded Nell's knowledge of fabric. She strolled into Jabberwocky Bookstore and wandered upstairs and down, glancing happily through books—none of them hers. Then she crossed the parking lot to the Newburyport Olive Oil Company and bought bottles of oil and balsamic vinegar, including a delectable new kind made with apricots. She spent more money on these bottles than she would have spent in a wine shop, but Nell allowed herself this luxury because she was in the chips.

Chapter 24

Brittany Baker stared down through the restaurant window at the savage currents of the Piscataqua River, snarling, reversing and surging against each other. Nell watched her watching.

"I wouldn't want to be in a kayak in that current," she ventured.

Brittany turned from the window.

"Nor would I," the young woman said. "But it is absorbing. Hard to draw the eyes away."

She did though and glanced around the restaurant, taking stock, as she sipped from her water glass. Nell wondered if it had been a mistake, coming all the way to Portsmouth to start the tour of the New England coast. But Surf offered an amazing view from its dining room and she'd been confident that this would be a good venue for stories to happen.

"*There is one story and one story only, that will prove worth your telling,*" she murmured, half to herself.

"What?"

"Robert Graves," Nell explained apologetically. "Sorry. It's a bad habit of mine—quoting obscure poems."

"Not so obscure," Brittany told her. "*Sorrow to sorrow as the sparks fly upward. The log groans and confesses: There is one story and one story only.*"

Nell stared. Brittany smiled.

"I was an English lit major at Northwestern."

"Ha," Nell said. "I am found out. Well, honesty being the best policy, I'll confess: I did bring you here hoping to hear your stories."

"My stories? I thought it was my great-grandparents' stories we were supposed to talk about."

"Well, yes, in the course of things. But I am hoping to get to know you. Your great-grandparents weren't able to supply much detail."

Brittany Baker looked at Nell gravely. Or suspiciously. Nell wasn't certain which. She had gray eyes, Nell saw. Clear gray eyes with the tiniest flecks of brown or gold. On one slender wrist she wore a gold chain no thicker than a strand of cobweb.

Tice and Bella Eton wished to learn about their heirs almost as much as they wanted to teach the young people about family, and Nell knew she was expected to mine information from the Greats and translate it for her clients. Winkling out stories was Nell's stock in trade, and she believed that conversation over a meal was one of the best ways to draw those stories forth. She was counting on food and drink and the atmosphere of Surf to do exactly that.

Brittany had been silent during most of the drive up Route 95, and thus far had revealed almost nothing of herself. Nell had to admit that the highway didn't offer much inducement to conversation. Just thirty or forty miles of wide pavement carved from trees and pastureland. Brittany had seemed at ease with the silence though. Most people felt responsible to fill every second with conversation—even at the cost of banality.

But Brittany, Nell had already decided, was amazingly self-contained.

"I thought we'd drive as far as Portsmouth, New Hampshire," Nell had explained. "It's a wonderful old working town. Tugboats on the river, great piles of salt and sand either off-loaded from barges or waiting to be loaded and shipped out—I can never tell which. Anyway, we'll have lunch and then head home along the seacoast. Very scenic. Maybe we'll stop in Newburyport on the way back and I can show you my little house. Then we'll follow the road around the rim of Cape Ann through Rockport and Gloucester and right back to Salem. I hope that sounds alright."

Nell's voice had sounded anxious to her own ears.

But Brittany had merely said, "It sounds fine" and gazed out the window at a field where Black Angus cattle grazed.

"What can I get you folks to drink?" The waitress was at the edge of the table. "Wine? Beer? Maybe a cocktail?"

Nell looked questioningly at Brittany.

"Just sparkling water with lime," Brittany said. Decisive. And quite specific, Nell thought.

"The same," Nell said, although she'd hoped a glass of wine would loosen the conversation and encourage some of Brittany's stories to emerge.

When the waitress had recited the specials and finally waddled off, Nell rested her elbow on the table, placed her chin on her fist and looked directly at Brittany, signaling her readiness to listen to whatever stories the young woman was willing to tell.

"Let's start at Northwestern. Since you're living in Chicago, I gather you decided to stay on after college? But what made you choose Northwestern?"

Brittany pursed her lips in thought.

"It seemed the diametric opposite of Atlanta."

Nell blinked. She raised her eyebrows to indicate she'd like elaboration.

Brittany shrugged.

"My parents live in Atlanta. I grew up there and I wanted to get the hell away. I filled out my application for Northwestern on a day when Chicago was crippled with a late spring snowstorm. In Atlanta, the magnolias were budding and on TV the weatherman was predicting a hot, steamy summer. Chicago seemed the antithesis of Atlanta and I thought: that's for me. Besides, I wanted to study English lit and Northwestern is academically credible. An exciting alternative to, let's say, Agnes Scott College."

"Atlanta's home," Nell observed. "Do you get back often?"

"Not often," Brittany said. "Only when absolutely necessary. I've established myself in Chicago and now that is home."

Nell, probing, guided her young guest through details of her job (marketing ... a big firm, solid ... good prospects for advancement ... yes, she liked the work very much.)

"Ever think of moving back to Atlanta?"

The question was innocent, but Brittany shot her a black look. It was the first crack in the calm that Nell had seen.

"No. Absolutely not. Listen, Mrs. Bane—Nell," she amended quickly "my experience of family is not all that pleasant. My parents don't like each other and they make that clear. My father is away most of the time 'on business' and my mother—Martha—has her own 'business'. Bridge club business, book club business, hairdresser business, the golf league, shopping... well, you get the picture. They should have divorced years ago but they stayed together for the child. That's me. I wish they hadn't."

Nell was silent. Now that the dam had opened she wasn't about to plug it up.

Brittany continued. "I suppose you could say my mother didn't have it all that easy. Her own mother—my grandmother Caroline Eton—died before Mom turned twenty. And it had just been the two of them for all the years Mom was growing up. No father because my grandparents split before Mom even got to kindergarten. I don't suppose Mom really knew how to have a family."

Brittany shook her head. "It's sad really."

And Nell had to agree. And into this tragic moment, their waitress reappeared bearing lunch and good cheer and, both women, eager to shift out of the descending mood, declared that the fish tacos looked delicious and told each other how hungry they were.

But over coffee, Nell reopened the subject.

"You suggested that your mother didn't really know how to have a family. And now, here you are in New England, visiting your great-grandparents and the reason you're here is because of family. Any thoughts about that?"

Brittany considered.

"Curiosity. As I've said, I haven't much experience of family. Not positive experience anyway. I wouldn't mind forging a connection. Also I'm told the Etons are quite wealthy. When you've lived by your wits—and often on Ramen Pride noodles—you are curious when you know that somewhere money is hanging on the family tree and perhaps some of it might flutter down to you."

"Well, that's an honest answer," Nell said. "I'll grant that."

And she slid her credit card back in her wallet and signed the tab.

"The afternoon is slipping away," she said. "Are you ready to drive along the rocky coast of your great-grandparents' New England? I'd love to show you my little antique cape in Newburyport."

Chapter 25

"I like your house. Do you live here alone?"

"I do, yes. But I didn't always."

Brittany, holding a glass of ice water, was standing in the middle of the kitchen. Interest animated her face as she spun to look at Nell.

"Ha," she said. "Your turn now. Tell."

So Nell told. Told about Lloyd and about the years where they parted slowly, so slowly, each year growing more painful. She told of the stamina it took to pursue the divorce and how, when it was all finally finished, she had opened up the kitchen just as she had felt she was opening up her soul.

"I knocked out a wall that blocked the kitchen from the snug, just there." Nell waved to indicate where the wall had been. "And I bumped out the back wall just a bit and inserted windows into every possible inch of space to bring in light. I finally felt there was light coming into my life. Light and fresh air. And I wrote an enormous check for this Aga just so I could simmer soup and fill the house with its fragrance. I make a lot of soup."

"Were you scared about managing on your own?" Brittany asked, studying Nell closely.

Nell considered this.

"Maybe. Maybe a little at first. But that really wasn't an issue when the alternative was to be buried alive—smothered—by a man who couldn't change. Couldn't open up. Not his fault, really; change was just beyond him."

Nell stopped apologetically.

"Well, it's hard to explain and I feel I am doing a botched job. But what it gets down to is this: this was my life. And I had to save it. I had to be who I am and who I was meant to be. Does that make any sense?"

Brittany was nodding.

"It does actually. It makes absolute sense."

She turned the glass between her hands, looking deeply into it.

"I think if my mother had been brave enough to do that, things would have been much better for her. For Dad, too actually. And probably for me."

She fell silent and Nell couldn't think of anything more to say. She had nothing to add to her biographical tale and she had the good sense not to insert consoling platitudes.

Brittany looked directly at Nell again.

"I'm pregnant."

Nell experienced several moments of confusion before she was able to bring out the words, "Congratulations. That must be exciting news indeed."

"To some, yes," Brittany said. "To me, yes. But not to everyone. I think the great-grandparents were horrified."

"You've told them then."

"Last night. At dinner. I think Prentice nearly choked. They immediately wanted to know about the father. When I told them it was immaterial because I wasn't planning to marry him—or anybody—they seemed very distressed. Prentice grew quite red in the face and I think Arabella was alarmed for him. She quickly changed the subject and there seemed to be a tacit agreement to say no more about it. At least not for the time being. But I'm pretty sure the subject isn't closed."

"So you're prepared to raise your child on your own," Nell said. "Well, it's certainly possible to be a single mother—and a good one—but it is difficult." Then she added hastily, "But listen to me telling you that! You've thought this out, I'm sure."

"I don't claim to have all the answers," Brittany said, "but you were on your own. And like you, I don't feel I have much choice. Eton women have a very bad track record with men."

"Would you care to explain that a bit more?"

"Well, take, my grandmother—Caroline—whom I never met incidentally. She took her three-year-old daughter and walked out on my grandfather and never looked back. She never remarried either. Apparently she was through with men before she turned twenty-five. Then my own mother—Martha— repeated the pattern with a few variations. Married my dad, stayed in a marriage that was unpleasant, to put it charitably. She lives unhappily in Atlanta, terrified that he'll walk out on her. Well, that's not what I want for myself. I want a family—yes! But I refuse to live like a scared mouse, dependent upon the whims of some guy. I am bright. Energetic. I have a career, and I can also have a home and a child."

Brittany spoke quietly, but her words vibrated with intensity.

"Choose life," Nell said simply. She was silent for a few moments, then scooped up her car keys.

"Well, if we're going to complete the tour of Cape Ann, we'd better get back into the car. Are you up for it?"

Brittany was.

Chapter 26

"So what is the future heiress like?" Bunty asked. She whapped a huge wad of clay onto a wooden board and didn't bother to look up.

"Attractive," Nell replied, cataloging. "Self-possessed. Independent. Self-contained. Intelligent. Well-mannered. Searingly honest. Pregnant..."

"Hold it!" Bunty commanded. "Right there! What was that last thing you said?"

"Pregnant?"

"That's the thing. Care to elaborate on that?"

Nell sighed.

"It was going so well," she said despondently. "I was looking forward to telling Bella and Tice that their great-granddaughter was everything they'd hoped. That her values were quite in line with theirs, except, as could be expected, those values were tempered to fit the twenty-first century. Then she dropped that verbal bomb."

"Do they know? The Etons, I mean."

"Oh, yes. She'd told them the night before our little jaunt. I gather they weren't thrilled. And for all the reasons you'd expect. She has no husband. Doesn't want a husband. Doesn't want any man messing up her life. She's determined to raise this child all on her own, thank you very much. Get out of my face, I'm just fine. And so on and so forth."

"Uh-oh," said Bunty.

"Well, you can hardly blame her," Nell said defensively. "She's never known any kind of typical, secure family life. Had a wounded mother—Martha—whose own mother—Caroline— gently checked out by committing suicide while Martha was still young. Martha'd never had a father present. I doubt she had any idea of the kind of family life that matched the Etons' model of normal. So Martha repeated her mother's pattern, except she never left her husband—just muddled along in a marriage that was dreary and unhappy with the result that her own daughter was miserable."

"And the Etons were too far removed to be involved," Bunty murmured, adding her own observation.

"True. So Brittany is determined not to repeat the pattern," Nell continued. "And I can see her point. On the other hand, I can see theirs as well. For the Etons, family values have been defined for generations by husband-wife-and-children around the dining table. Dinner at noon on Sundays after church with extended family all around. It will be a stretch for them to accept, let alone approve of, Brittany's choice."

Bunty returned to her clay. She peeled up the wad, turned it, and whapped again. Nell winced.

"Why are you doing that?"

Bunty applied the heels of her hands to the clay and pushed.

"You have to get the air bubbles out."

Nell watched for a while.

"So what's up now?" Bunty grunted as she kneaded.

"Brittany is leaving tomorrow," Nell replied. "I'm going down to Salem to help see her off."

"And also to see how the doting great-grandparents are doing?"

"That as well."

Chapter 27

Frank Largent had parked Brittany's rented Ford in the courtyard and now he maneuvered Tice's wheelchair down the back ramp.

"I woulda brought down your bags for you," he told Brittany, "only you didn't seem to have any."

"Just this." Brittany held up her carry-on, "And I can easily manage it myself."

Nell stood with Bella, Tice, Frank and Henny, all lined up to say goodbye. Like a reverse receiving line, Nell thought.

As well as her shoulder bag and carry-on, Brittany was clutching her copy of *Looking Forward*. She stood in front of her great-grandparents.

"I will write to you after I get back to Chicago," she told them. "By then I hope to have found the words to say what this book means to me. It is an amazing thing and very possibly the most meaningful gift I've ever received from family."

"Oh, my dear child!"

This was all Bella could manage and her voice broke on

the last word. But she held her arms wide and Brittany flung herself into them, resting her head for a moment on her great-grandmother's shoulder.

She turned to Tice who, looking stern, took her hand in both of his and gently pulled her down closer to his level as he delivered a lecture meant to be stern, although in that, it didn't succeed.

"You are to stay in touch," he instructed her. "Let us know how you and your child are doing. And if we can help in any way..." and here the old man swung Brittany's arm back and forth..."in *any* way—you are to let us know immediately. Do you understand?"

His eyes were steely. Brittany returned his look.

"Yes, I do understand. And I will know that you are there for me—for us—and that will be of immense reassurance. And I *will* stay in touch. That is a promise."

Mollified, Tice released her hand. He nodded twice. Brittany turned to Nell. The two women looked levelly at each other for several moments. Then suddenly Brittany was in Nell's arms too.

"Thank you for all you've done for my great-grandparents," Brittany whispered in Nell's ear. "You've helped them realize an amazing dream. And you've helped me as well. Now you must stay in touch with me!"

"That's a promise," Nell whispered back.

Henny and Frank each had a turn at hugging Brittany, and then with a flash of lovely thigh, she was into the car and at the wheel of the little Ford Focus. The motor started, there was a quick wave and a short toot-toot of the horn and Brittany Baker, one of the heirs to the Eton fortune, turned onto North Federal Square and was gone.

The little group, perhaps feeling diminished, continued to stand in the courtyard, taking in the fact of Brittany's leaving.

Then Frank slowly turned the wheelchair and pushed Tice up the ramp with Henny following closely.

Bella and Nell turned too.

"Tice looks a bit tired, I think," Nell said.

"Yes, I'm afraid he is. The news of the baby was hard for him to hear. On one hand the advent of a first great-great-grandchild is wonderful news but Tice is having great difficulty accepting the decisions Brittany has made. They violate the values that have guided and informed his entire life."

"And you, Bella?" Nell asked, "Where do you stand?"

But Arabella Eton refused to meet either Nell's eyes or her question.

Chapter 28

Nell, waiting to see the late news, was losing the battle to keep her eyelids open, but when the phone rang—startlingly loud— they snapped up like window shades. She sat bug-eyed for several seconds. Who could be calling at this unconscionable hour?

"Sorry to call so late," said Robert Hutchins, "but I thought I'd better give you a heads up."

"Oh, Robert, you gave me a fright! Is everything alright? Has someone been injured?"

"Nothing like that," Robert said drily, "but I have just come home from collecting Indigo Eton from the airport and delivering her into the care of her great-grandparents. Knowing you are going to North Federal Square for lunch tomorrow, I though I'd brace you. The girl has blue hair."

"Blue?" Nell was bewildered.

"She explained that she tries to live up to her name."

"Indigo. I see. Oh dear."

"Well, have a delightful lunch," Robert said. "Call me afterwards."

Nell was pretty sure she heard him chuckle just before he clicked off the line. But now she was awake. Wide awake. And she knew sleep was several hours off. So she finished watching the late news and switched off the television. But once in bed, she found she was still wide awake, and after tossing for a half hour and turning her pillow over five times trying to get a cool surface to lay her face upon, she slipped into an uncomfortable sleep and dreamed of weird creatures with blue hair.

Chapter 29

"Crystal was born in a yurt," Indigo said abruptly into the gentle luncheon conversation. The statement was punctuated with a slurp of soup. "Up in the High Sierras without a midwife or nothing, just her old man to catch her."

The other three, startled, looked up from their soup.

"Do you even know what a yurt is?" she demanded witheringly.

Into the surprised silence, Nell offered mildly, "I believe a yurt is a circular dwelling originating in the steppes of central Asia."

Indigo stared at her.

Nell meekly dipped her spoon into her soup. The girl continued to examine Nell with her somewhat prominent gaze. Her eyes were like grapes, Nell decided. Green grapes. Indigo applied herself to her soup bowl. Tomato bisque with Chantilly cream. Delicious. Nell discerned a hint of clove. There was another slurp.

Arabella winced.

Tice gallantly tried to follow the conversational direction the girl had pointed.

"Tell us about your parents, Indigo. We haven't seen them for quite some time. What are they up to?"

Indigo turned to her great-grandfather.

"Mikey and Crystal?"

"Is that what you call your parents? Mikey and Crystal?"

"Those are their names, right?"

She turned her grape-green gaze fully upon her great-grandfather.

"Mikey says you're rich," she told him. "He says we have to be nice to you."

Helplessly, Prentice Eton made a silent appeal down the table to his wife, but before Bella could take control of the conversation on his behalf, Indigo continued.

"Mikey's so thick. Geez, he does everything Crystal tells him to do. Hasn't got a mind of his own, that one."

Tice laid his spoon down next to his bowl and patted his lips with his napkin. His face had reddened considerably. Bella, seeing he was upset, hurried to smooth things over.

"Perhaps Mrs. Bane would like to tell us her plans for your visit, Indigo."

Nell took the cue and slid in smoothly. "I hope you'll call me Nell, Indigo, since we're going to be... friends."

She'd meant to stabilize the conversation with this offer, but Nell suddenly realized it was the subject of first names that had put this conversation into the weeds to start with. Well, too late. She blundered on.

"Your family, Indigo, has a long history here in Salem, so I thought we'd do the town."

She saw that dated allusion was lost on the girl.

"We'll start with the Peabody Essex Museum, see the Customs House, tour the House of Seven Gables."

Indigo regarded her with a flat stare.

"Maybe even see the Witch Museum and a couple of the shops. How does that sound?"

Indigo shrugged and reapplied herself to her soup.

"Whatever."

Although Robert Hutchins had tried to prepare Nell for Indigo's appearance, he hadn't gone far enough. Nell had imagined one of those blue rinses little old ladies order in beauty parlors to brighten their white hair, but Indigo's blue looked like she had applied enamel to her head with a wide, flat brush. It was lacquer-stiff and the color of a Solo cup. The application mystified Nell as well. The girl had made no attempt to paint her entire head, so plenty of her own blonde hair was still evident under the enamel. She'd painted her bitten nails blue as well and a number of her many ear piercings sported blue stones. She had a small sapphire at the crest of one nostril.

Nell smiled bravely.

"I thought we'd being our adventure right after lunch."

"Whatever," said Indigo Eton.

"Slurp."

Chapter 30

Victoria Station was Nell's inspired choice for dinner with Indigo Eton. They would be shown to a table by one of the big windows, Nell imagined, one with a view of Salem Harbor and of people strolling past the umbrella-topped tables on the wharf. Not too fussy or upscale, Nell thought; just the right amount of casual, local color.

She felt drained by the time she and Indigo were shown to that table by the window though. The chair the host held for her was unbelievably welcome and she sank down, grateful to be off her feet at last.

"A Coke," said Indigo when the waiter offered to take their drinks order.

"Iced tea, please," responded Nell, "unsweetened."

She sat back and beamed at her companion, ready for their first real face-to-face chat. But Indigo, with her elbow on the table and her cheek mashed against her fist, was gazing around the restaurant with those bulging grape-green eyes. A young woman with long black hair and a low-cut shirt that invited a stunning view of an elaborate butterfly tattooed on her sternum—its brilliant wings spreading across her collarbones—caught Indigo's eye.

"Look at that ink!" Indigo breathed, more to herself than to Nell, and riveted, she stared at the butterfly woman's hip-swiveling progress through the restaurant among the tables.

Nell had to clear her throat three times to pull Indigo's attention back to their table. The girl's mouth was slightly ajar.

"Hello," Nell said, snapping her fingers a couple of times. "Nell Bane here."

She had the sense that Indigo didn't quite recognize her.

Indigo reluctantly allowed her attention to be pulled toward Nell's snapping fingers. Nell smiled and spread her napkin on her lap.

"Well," she said. "You've certainly seen a lot of Salem today. What did you think? What are your impressions?"

Indigo gave a final, longing look in the direction of the butterfly woman who had taken a seat on the other side of the restaurant. She had to rotate her head nearly 270 degrees to accomplish this, and she turned back to Nell with something like resignation. Okay. This was what she was going to have to do—make small talk with this boring woman. Indigo sighed and appeared to think.

"Ah... it's okay, I guess." Then she brightened. "The witch shop was awesome! That place with the geodes and all the silver jewelry, that was pretty good too."

Nell nodded encouragingly.

"What did you think of the museum?"

Indigo thought some more. Trying to recall the museum apparently.

"It was okay. I liked that big room with the carved people."

"The figureheads from old sailing ships," Nell supplied.

"Whatever."

Indigo looked around again. Nell persevered.

"Are you enjoying your visit with your great-grandparents?"

Nell mentally scolded herself for this dull conversational gambit. Next I'll be asking what grade she's in at school, she thought.

A shrug was the answer. Nell tried again.

"Your visit is very important to your great-grandparents, Indigo. They are eager to get to know you, but they are also very keen to put you in touch with your family and your roots."

"With Mikey and Crystal?"

"Well, that is your family, of course, but I was talking about your more extended family. Prentice and Arabella want you to see where your grandparents lived as children. And they want you to see—and to appreciate—the things that are important to them. The museum for one thing. They have contributed a great deal to make the museum what it is. In fact though, they've built things that aren't just bricks and mortar. Intangibles. There are a number of social causes here in Salem and in Boston that have been greatly enriched by their philanthropy."

Nell saw Indigo's jaw elongate as she tried to swallow a yawn. Nell gave her a point for swallowing.

The waiter appeared.

"Have you decided?" Nell asked the girl.

"A hamburger," Indigo announced. "And can we get a plate of those boathouse nachos?"

The waiter and Nell both indicated this was possible, and Nell ordered butternut ravioli. The butterfly woman was on the move again, this time with her companion. Indigo watched them leave.

"Do you have any tattoos?" Nell asked.

Indigo shrugged dismissively. "Just insignificant ones. I'd

like something really awesome though. Statement ink. But Crystal—God! Ink is expensive and Crystal'd make me pay for it myself."

Indigo's indignant expression invited Nell to share this outrage. Nell lifted her eyebrows in what she hoped was a sympathetic validation. Had Indigo been her daughter, however, Nell would have had several things to say—all of them crisper than Crystal's point.

Now the waiter appeared with a flourish and set a huge plate of boathouse nachos on the table between them. Indigo immediately pulled a nacho off the top of the stack and oblivious to the trail of melted cheese, bit into it, chewing noisily.

"Help yourself," she offered magnanimously, and Nell, with a sense of irony—after all, she was the one paying for this— obediently selected a nacho from an area of the platter where the cheese was thinner.

"Oh!" she exclaimed, "Hot!"

Indigo laughed. "The temperature or the jalapeno? In California, we're used to hot food."

And as if to prove this, Indigo shoved another nacho into her mouth and crunched.

Over the main course, Nell tried once more to edge Indigo back to the subject of family.

"I understand your great-grandparents gave you a copy of their memoir the night you arrived."

"A what?"

"Memoir. *Looking Forward.* Their book."

"Oh. Oh, yeah."

Indigo lifted her hamburger with both hands, took a bite and chewed thoughtfully. With her mouth open. Nell looked away.

"I helped them write it," Nell said desperately. "They told

me their stories and I wrote them down. They want you and your brother and your cousin Brittany to know as much as possible about your ancestors and about the values your great-grandparents hold as important."

As Nell watched, Indigo's gaze drifted from the table and she scanned the restaurant once more, possibly looking for more significant ink—design ideas to use on the day she could get ahold of enough money for a really awesome tattoo.

Indigo suddenly instigated conversation.

"Mikey says my great-grandparents are rich."

She said this around half-chewed hamburger and looked expectantly at Nell for confirmation.

"They are wealthy, yes."

Indigo seemed to be thinking, and Nell decided to pursue the subject.

"If you were wealthy, what would you do? Would you do as your great-grandparents have and endow some social or cultural cause? Give some of it to charity?"

Indigo thought some more. This involved pulling a French fry out of the stack beside her hamburger and consuming it slowly from one end down to her fingertips.

"I would—yeah. I'd set up a charity for homeless animals. Cats and like that."

If she was expecting disapproval from Nell, she didn't get it.

"That would qualify as charitable," Nell told the girl. "What else?"

Indigo sighed blissfully and sat back in her chair.

"I'd buy some really excellent flash! Something like that butterfly!"

With a sigh, Nell gave up and cut into a ravioli with the side of her fork. This evening too, like all things, would pass.

Chapter 31

"It wasn't a success, Robert," Nell sighed the next day when she made her report to Robert Hutchins. "Bella's fresh tomato bisque was delicious but after lunch, the day went downhill. And rapidly."

"She's a graceless girl," Robert agreed. "And she seems immature for seventeen. I didn't envy you the chore of squiring her around Salem. How did it go?"

"I had planned the afternoon so carefully, starting at the Peabody Essex. I explained that her great-grandparents were patrons of the museum—and that they had contributed significantly to it and were justifiably proud of it. And I tried to paint a picture for her of the dusty old place it once was— nothing but figureheads from sailing ships and Essex dories. Then I pointed out the soaring Safdie architecture with its wonderful ship-like referents. But I might as well have walked through the place with an automaton. No comments. She hardly looked at anything. I got the impression her eyes weren't even focused, and she barely responded when I called her attention to something or asked her a direct question. 'Whatever', seems to be the comment that covers all occasions."

Nell sighed but continued.

"The Customs House was no more successful. I've always thought that view down the causeway from the front window is spectacular. And I thought she'd be excited to realize that her ancestors probably sat in that very place and looked up from their ledgers to see the same sights she was seeing. But no. Apparently not."

Robert made a sympathetic sound and Nell plunged on.

"The House of Seven Gables—well, she started shifting from foot to foot and making these loud sighs while the guide was talking. She let everybody know how terrifically bored she was. I was embarrassed."

"Weren't there any successes?" Robert asked sympathetically.

"Yes. That new age shop on Derby Street—the one that sells crystals and incense and Tarot cards. She loved that place. I thought I'd never get the smell of patchouli out of my sinuses. Since I'd had a fragment of success there though, we went over to Laurie Cabot's shop and Indigo fingered all the witch paraphernalia. I have to say she fit right in."

Nell sighed and continued.

"Then, to wrap it up, we had dinner at Pickering Wharf. Had a window right on the water. She ordered a hamburger. Apparently she was never taught to chew with her mouth closed. I dropped her off with Etons about eight o'clock and went home with a headache. Oh Robert, I feel terrible for Tice and Bella. Whatever are they going to do with her for the rest of the visit?"

"They've only got a day and a half to go," Robert said consolingly. "Then I'll pick up Indigo and drive her back to Logan to catch her plane."

"Well the day wasn't a total loss," Nell sighed. "I got Henny to give me recipe for that fresh tomato bisque."

FRESH TOMATO SOUP
4 – 5 large, fresh tomatoes, skins removed and coarsely chopped
1/2 cup minced onion or shallot
1/4 cup chopped celery with leaves
2 Tbl butter
2 Tbl flour
2 cups whole milk or light cream
1/2 t sugar
1/4 t paprika
1/4 ground cloves
1 Tb chopped fresh basil

Nell gently cooked the shallots and celery in a saucepan just long enough to soften them. Next she added the tomatoes, covered the pan and simmered the vegetables for 15 minutes. She strained the mixture, reserving the tomato stock in one bowl and the vegetables in another. Melting the butter in the saucepan, she used the flour to make a roux, then added 1 cup of the tomato stock. Finally she added back the reserved tomato, shallot and celery along with the milk. When the soup had just come to a simmer, it was ready for a garnish of chopped basil leaves and a dollop of sour cream or yogurt.

Chapter 32

Bunty Whitney was keeping score. "Two down," she said, "and one to go. When is the male heir arriving?"

"Next week," Nell said. "Tice and Bella are resting up for the visit, but Tice is so excited he can hardly stand it. This young man—Derek—is going to carry on the Eton name and Tice has great plans to discuss the responsibilities and ramifications of this with him. It is an honor and an obligation apparently. The girls are one thing, but Tice is enough of an old-fashioned patriarch to care passionately about perpetuating the Eton name."

"What if he's like his sister Indigo?"

Bunty was playing devil's advocate.

"That would be practically impossible. Nobody could be that louche. Do you know what Tice said when she'd left? 'Thank God that boring child has gone back to California!' So sad. He—they—had such high hopes for their great-grandchild."

"It must say something about the parents though," Bunty

said. "The apple doesn't fall far from the tree. Listen, I have to take an order of mugs over to a shop in Rockport. Want to come and help me carry a carton?"

Nell was glad of the chance to do something other than prepare for—or recover from—the Eton family business. And next week would come soon enough. And when it came, it would bring Derek Eton with it. For better or for worse. In the meantime a trip to Rockport might be just the ticket. And after the business of delivering Bunty's mugs, perhaps they could have the pleasure of a stroll down Bearskin Neck.

But driving back to Newburyport near the end of their field trip, Bunty reopened the subject.

"So what's the plan for young Master Eton? And what's the tune you'll be dancing to?"

Nell leaned her head back against the passenger's seat and closed her eyes the better to recall the itinerary the Etons had planned for her and Robert Hutchins.

"Let's see. He's arriving on Thursday and taking a limo out to Salem. Robert and I will get to meet him on Friday night when we are invited for dinner. By that time, Derek and his great-grandparents will have had a chance to get to know each other over a twenty-four hour stretch of time. On Saturday, Derek is taking the train to Boston and Robert and Jerry Gasso are going to show him all the sights. And Sunday it's my turn. I'll see if there is anything still unseen in Salem—if he hasn't been to the PEM on his own, I'll certainly take him there. Then we'll drive up the coast and around Cape Ann, much like the tour I did with Brittany except in reverse, and I'll have him home by evening. He leaves for California on Monday and life gets back to normal, I expect."

Bunty drove without comment for a half mile.

"Then your work with the Etons is done," she summarized.

"Yes," Nell agreed. "Then, all the hurley-burley's done."

Chapter 33

Nell had her head in her closet and truth to tell she was feeling a bit nervous.

"This is stupid!" she told herself sharply. "I am simply going to dinner at the home of friends. I am just going to meet a twenty-year-old boy. What's all this about?"

But she'd been standing in front of her closet for at least ten minutes, pulling at hems and matching them against other garments. She'd yanked—oh, who knew how many hangers off the clothes bar and pressed half dozen outfits against her front while gazing with distaste into the mirror.

"Bother!" she said. Then, "The hell with it!'

She pulled out a summer dress at random.

"You're it," she told it. "We're stepping out to dinner together."

She slipped into the dress, zipped it, found some shoes, combed her hair and applied lipgloss. Then she drove to Salem.

It took some moments for Arabella Eton to answer her ring at the front door. Nell leaned in to give Bella's cheek a peck.

"Is he here then? Did he arrive in good nick?"

"Oh yes," Bella said. "Derek is fine, but poor Frank isn't."

Nell was instantly solicitous.

"Frank Largent? What's wrong?"

"Bronchitis. And strep throat. Poor fellow! I had to speak quite sharply to get him off to the doctor. He kept protesting that we—especially Tice—couldn't manage without him. Then Henny, bless her, stepped in and read the 'Now hear this!' loud and clear. 'Frank Largent,' she said, 'your first order of business is to get well! Then you can get back to the business of seeing after Tice. But so help me Hannah,' she said, 'if you give that bronchitis germ to Tice, why that'll...that could just finish him!'"

Bella permitted herself a small chuckle even though she still looked worried.

"Henny and I swore we could manage Tice and if there was any heavy work to do—transfers, that sort of thing—why we'd have a strong young man in the house. Derek would be more than pleased to give his great-grandfather a hand."

"So Frank is out in his apartment in the carriage house resting?" Nell whispered.

"No," Bella whispered back, "he went down to his sister's house in Quincy. She's a licensed practical nurse and she's insisted on keeping an eye on him."

"And very wise too," Nell whispered, adding "Why are we whispering?"

"I have no idea," Arabella said briskly. "Do come. Let me take your sweater. Do come through and meet Derek."

Nell did just that. Robert Hutches instantly rose to his feet as Nell entered the living room, although Tice, of course, couldn't rise and Derek Eton didn't. Prentice Eton threw a meaningful look in the young man's direction—a look that Derek either didn't receive or ignored.

"Nell! How good to see you. Come in, come in and meet our great-grandson. This is Derek…"

At this point Tice aimed an even more compelling look at the young man sprawled in the room's most comfortable chair and sitting on the very base of his spine with his long legs splayed out in front. This time Derek Eton took the hint and slowly, as if every muscle were resisting, pulled himself upright. The hand he offered Nell to shake felt like last week's lettuce. In contrast, Nell grasped his hand firmly. A good, strong handshake was essential, she believed. Give a good pressure that stops short of pain and look 'em right in the eye.

"Having heard so much about you," she smiled, "I have naturally been very eager to meet you. This is indeed a pleasure."

"How'd ya do," Derek said. It was not a question.

"What can I get you to drink, Nell?" Robert, as *in loco* host, asked.

Nell took a quick inventory of beverages—Robert and Tice had short glasses of scotch and Derek had beer. In a bottle.

"Wine would be lovely. Any sort of white."

"Wine for you as well, Bella? Or would you prefer sherry?" Robert asked.

"Now," said Tice decisively, when the ladies held glasses, "we were talking, Nell, of the museum. Bringing young Derek here up to speed on the transformation that has taken place in the last years."

Nell turned enthusiastically to the young man and was shocked to see an affect of complete boredom, of which Prentice in his enthusiasm, was apparently, unaware. The old man went on chatting amiably about one of his favorite subjects while Nell cast about in her mind to find a topic mutually appealing to Derek Eton and his great-grandfather.

"You probably haven't had much opportunity to explore

Salem yet," she told him, "but I wonder—have you had the chance to walk about? See the museum from the outside? See the wharves? The Common?"

"Yeah. Sort of. I strolled around some this afternoon. There are a lot of pretty shabby places around here, aren't there? Those ramshackle tenements a couple streets over—families living on all three floors—they look pretty grubby."

Tice looked dumfounded. Bella looked disturbed. Robert Hutchins cut in smoothly.

"Salem is an old town, Derek. A number of houses here date back to the seventeen and eighteen-hundreds. I would imagine that much of the architecture around here looks dramatically different from what you're used to seeing in California?"

He smiled invitingly as he offered this bit of white flag that Derek should have the good sense to grasp and thus bridge the awkwardness of his earlier statement.

In answer, Derek gave Robert an extended stare and took a long pull on his bottle of beer. Silence lay in the room.

Then, mercifully, Henny sailed in. "Dinner is all ready!" she chirped. "I hope everyone likes salmon, and the asparagus is local. It's lovely!"

"I understand you are at Berkeley." Robert Hutchins addressed Derek pleasantly over the soup course. "What is your field?"

"I haven't declared yet," Derek replied. "I see myself as more of a Renaissance type—well-versed in a number of disciplines. So I'm sort of conducting an academic audition. A bit of philosophy here, a smattering of political science there, looking in on the School of Social Welfare—that sort of thing. Evaluating what the school does best. Designing my own curriculum."

He turned to Arabella.

"The soup is cold, by the way."

"It's vichyssoise," she told him. "It's usually served chilled and it's one of Tice's favorites. Do you like it?"

"It's okay, I guess. I never ate cold soup."

"It is delicious," Nell volunteered. "Just a dusting of mace and a scattering of chive. Perfect!"

Arabella looked gratified. Robert, determined to pursue his original thought, continued as though the soup interlude had never happened.

"The well-rounded man. Yes. A good liberal arts background is never wasted. But you are—what?—two years into your studies now? What is beginning to appeal?"

"The social welfare stuff is sort of interesting. That's what struck me when I saw those tenements just beyond that big green park you call the Common."

He addressed his great-grandfather.

"I can't see how you can justify living in this big house— which obviously cost a packet-and-a-half, by the way—when people a few blocks away are so obviously in financial need. Don't you two have any kind of social conscience?"

He turned to include Arabella at the other end of the table as he said this.

The accusation—so outrageous and so unfair—was left to Robert Hutchins to defend. In a choked voice he described some of the charitable interests that the Etons supported.

"Tice and Bella participate generously in a number of charitable efforts, both here in Salem and in Boston. HAWK, for instance, is one example; it assists homeless and abused women," Robert said. "And to name just a few others, there's Planned Parenthood, the local food pantry and their own church right here in Salem."

Derek snorted.

"Church doesn't count!" he said shortly. "And writing a

check! When you have a lot of money, sitting down and dashing off the occasional check is easy. And it's about as effective spitting in the ocean."

"See here, young man..." Tice started.

But Robert interrupted, his voice dangerously low and quiet. Nell had never heard him use such a tone.

"Your great-grandparents are elderly, Derek. And yes, now much of their social and cultural support involves writing checks. Extremely generous ones. However, they've spent their active years lending muscle as well as money to good causes. When you read their memoir, you'll come to understand the long history of social conscience that has informed their interests and actions. You'll read how your great-grandmother's family took in evacuees during World War II. You'll read of her support of the Planned Parenthood League, which in the 'forties and 'fifties put her at some risk since contraception was illegal here in Massachusetts. And you'll read of the great sacrifice for his country that your great-grandfather made as a soldier in World War II. He put off personal plans and professional interests to devote five years to military service. He put his life on the line and demonstrated his willingness to lay down his life for this country."

For the taciturn Robert Hutchins, this was quite a speech.

Nell was impressed. But Derek Eton wasn't.

"War!" Derek spat the word. "That's what your generation always comes back to. The greatest generation! The war to end all wars. Well, WWII didn't do that, did it? End wars? More wars keep coming. Well, what about peace? My other grandparents—my mother's people on the Coast—were part of the early peace movement. They marched. Demonstrated. Kept at it even while the pigs were clubbing them and hauling them off to jail. They kept marching and shouting. Why, the country would still be crawling around Vietnam if the peace movement hadn't pointed out the stupidity of the war and brought it to an end. That's what ended Vietnam, you know. The peaceniks shamed the country and the government into declaring victory and slinking home."

An appalled silence enveloped the table. Derek Eton scraped the last of the vichyssoise from his bowl and laid down his spoon. Then an aproned angel of mercy in the form of Henny DeFelice appeared and began collecting the soup plates. Nell rose to give her a hand. In the kitchen she found Henny stacking the plates in a fury.

"It's been like this all day," she hissed. "They've been at each other every minute. Grizzling like schoolboys. There isn't a single thing they seem able to agree on and that smug young man seems poised every second to take another bite out of his great-grandfather!"

Henny shook her head and handed Nell two plates of pink salmon partnered with perfectly steamed asparagus.

"Carry those in, dear, then sit down and pray for peace during the main course," she said.

Nell placed one of the plates before Bella and the other in front of Derek. He looked down.

"I hate asparagus and I don't eat fish."

It would, Nell reflected grimly, take more than prayer to bring peace to this table.

The sniping and arguing continued in the living room after dinner. Bella, Nell and Robert, like vigilant border collies, kept trying to turn the conversation to kinder, gentler topics, but as soon as one of them managed this, Prentice or Derek wrenched the conversation back into turbulence. Nell was surprised. She had never seen Tice so inflamed. The kind, smiling man she thought she knew so well had been taken over—possessed—by an old man struggling valiantly to assert and defend the things he so passionately believed in. And

Derek, really! He should have been more sensitive. To actually pick fights with the great-grandfather he scarcely knew...well! This was certainly the time for polite containment, Nell thought. It served no good purpose to deliberately goad the old gentleman.

"How old are you?" Tice demanded of Derek.

"Twenty."

Tice gave him a long, searching look.

"Twenty. The same age as Spike Caldecott when his life ended in an M-4 Sherman tank."

The old man shook his head.

"I can't see you taking on the responsibility Spike had. Responsibility for other men's lives and the willingness to give life for country."

"I can't see myself in that position either," Derek retorted. "I'd have had more sense. War is senseless. To glorify it, as your generation did—you guys who fought in World War II— is obscene."

And they were off on that terrible subject once more. Nell, forced to listen, felt her stomach and chest tighten painfully.

The interminable evening ended at last and Nell was grateful to be released into the pleasant summer night.

"Oh, Robert," she sighed, as then stepped side by side down the granite steps, "what an opinionated young man! This doesn't bode well for the visit, and I certainly don't envy you tomorrow, having to squire Derek Eton around Boston."

"I'm viewing it as a mission of mercy," Robert said. "Perhaps when he is away from Tice he'll reveal a less abrasive element of his personality. In any case, a day away from here will give Tice and Bella the chance to rest and recover."

"Or perhaps not," said Nell crisply.

"We'll see," said Robert Hutchins. "And by the way," he added as they parted to go to their individual cars, "you're not off the hook either. Sunday is your day to babysit."

Chapter 34

Nell had a Saturday morning guest for coffee. Bunty Whitney strolled into Nell's kitchen at eight o'clock, carrying her own mug of coffee and grinning expectantly.

"Well? What's he like, this young heir apparent?"

"To be perfectly honest, Bunty, he's not long on charm."

Since attending the book signing party, Bunty had become deeply interested in the Etons' drama. She had read her copy of *Looking Forward* from cover to cover and had insisted that Nell sign the flyleaf right below Arabella Eton's perfect Palmer method signature.

"What does he look like? Blue hair?"

"Of course not." Nell considered. "I did expect him to resemble Indigo, though. You know, not fat really but sort of puffy. He isn't bad looking. Not really handsome, but I think he could be if he weren't so disagreeable."

And Nell described the evening's conversation for Bunty, who shuddered.

"What do you make of it, Bunty? Why would a young man

who has been invited to the other side of the country to visit the great-grandparents he's never met—family of considerable means who have demonstrated an interest in him—why would he be so immediately and so intentionally rude?"

Bunty lifted her coffee mug to her lips and held it there without sipping.

"Defense mechanism, perhaps? Congenital rudeness? It is possible that the young man resents people who have more money than he has. In other words, he may have scarcity issues—if you have all the money, then there's not enough left for me. You've got it all and it isn't fair!"

Nell protested. "But that doesn't make sense," she argued.

"Doesn't have to," Bunty said. "None of these defense mechanisms are sensible. They are merely perceptions—or misperceptions. Then there's always the distant possibility that Derek Eton is simply expressing his true feelings and impressions and simply doesn't care if he hurts someone's feelings. Maybe he believes implicitly in his own 'rightness'? I really can't say. But I will stay tuned."

Nell shook her head.

"I find myself dreading tomorrow. You know how there are some people whose company you avoid? People who seem wrapped in a negative energy? Well, that's how Derek Eton feels to me. Negative. And his energy drains the good feelings right out of me. Makes me dark and depressed and argumentative as well. I don't like myself much when I'm around him, and every instinct tells me to stay away."

Bunty was sympathetic.

"Nothing to do, I guess, but go forward," she offered. "But let tomorrow's troubles be sufficient to the day thereof. No sense in poisoning today. It's a lovely Saturday. How are you going to spend it?"

"Bella served a delicious vichyssoise last night," Nell

replied. "I'm going to make my own batch.

NELL'S VICHYSSOISE
3 medium leeks, washed and thinly sliced
1 medium onion, chopped
2 T butter
4 medium russet potatoes, peeled and sliced paper-thin
4 cups chicken stock
1-1/2 cups of light cream
1/4 tsp mace fresh chives for garnish

Nell sautéed the onion and leek in the butter. Then she added the potatoes and stock and simmered until the potato was tender. She used the immersion blender to thoroughly puree the mixture and set it in the refrigerator to chill. Just before serving, she stirred in the cream and mace and sprinkled chopped chive on top.

Chapter 35

"*Half a league, half a league, half a league onward,*" intoned Nell, pressing on the accelerator. Then, "Hell's bum!"

The cell phone on the seat beside her chimed, interrupting *The Charge of the Light Brigade.* She was bound for Salem and her assigned day with Derek Eton, and she didn't like talking on the cell while driving. Do it once—pick up just once—and that's the moment a cop is going to pull abreast, glance over and see you breaking the law. It chimed again.

"Hell's bum!" she repeated, snatching up the instrument. "Yes! What?"

But Robert Hutchins didn't hear the vexation in her tone. "Thank God I reached you!"

There was relief in Robert's voice but a layer of urgency too. Without waiting, he rushed on.

"I wanted to reach you before you got all the way to Salem. Tice has had some kind of episode—a stroke most probably. Henny called 911 then called me. The ambulance is on the way to Lahey North Shore and I'm heading there now."

"I'm almost at the turn-off," Nell told him. "I'll meet you there if that's alright."

"I was hoping you would," Robert said. "You'll probably arrive before I do and I'm terribly worried about Bella. She'll need someone with her. I'll get there as fast as I can."

Nell clicked off the cell and pressed harder on the accelerator. In minutes she saw the sign for Lahey Clinic and on the rise behind the hospital saw the North Shore Mall, glinting in the sun like some pale, modern Oz. Instead of taking the exit all the way to Route 114, she dipped below the highway and entered the vast parking lot, turning toward Lahey.

Arabella Eton and Henny DeFelice were huddled together on a pair of unforgiving chairs in the emergency room. Henny indicated a curtained cubicle.

"He's in there."

"How is he?" whispered Nell.

"We don't know," Bella said very softly. "He's not conscious and the doctors haven't said anything definite."

"Do you know what happened?" Nell asked.

"Not really. We found him slumped in his wheelchair in his bedroom this morning. Derek had been in there a while before. They were talking. Derek said Tice was sleeping when he left the room."

Arabella's pretty face was sagging with anxiety.

"We didn't waste much time in conversation. Just rushed to get the ambulance. Robert?"

Bella looked around helplessly.

"He's on the way," Nell assured her quickly. "He called me from his car and caught me just before I got off 95. I was practically at the hospital's door."

Bella patted Nell's hand.

"I'm glad you're here, dear."

But she continued to peer down the corridor. Then at last,

there came Robert, striding on his long legs. Moving rapidly. Bella's face relaxed into relief. Robert Hutchins folded Arabella into his arms and held her for a long time. Then he opened an arm to make room for Henny and held her too. Robert, Nell knew, was not a demonstrative man but she understood how much Prentice and Arabella meant to him.

"Have they . . . ? Do they . . .?"

Nell shook her head.

"Nothing yet. No word really beyond the report that they are trying to stabilize him and time will tell. Time, apparently, is our friend here. He isn't conscious but the longer he lasts, the better are his chances."

"I see." Robert sighed.

It was a day of waiting. And a day of weariness interrupted by spikes of adrenalin when a doctor strode past or a nurse, with a rattle of beads, drew back a curtain.

At some point in the afternoon, Tice was transferred to ICU, and Robert and Bella, Henny and Nell trailed along and adjusted themselves to a new waiting room. The room outside ICU, though, was more gracious than the ER—the lights dimmer, the chairs softer. Henny telephoned the house on North Federal Square where Derek Eton was alone. She reported on his great-grandfather's condition (unknown but reasonably stable) and described the foods in the pantry and refrigerator that might appeal to him.

A doctor entered the waiting room and asked for Mrs. Eton. Robert was immediately on his feet and the physician, who introduced himself as Dr. Mesardjian, came and sat in the chair next to Bella and took her hand. At a louder-than-necessary volume and in a slower-than-necessary cadence, he explained that Mr. Eton's vital signs were still wavering a bit but there was reason to hope they would stabilize during the night. No, he hadn't yet regained consciousness, so it was difficult to establish the extent of damage this second stroke had caused. Dr. Mesardjian thought it would be wise for Mrs. Eton to go home. Get some rest. She could come back in the morning and perhaps there would be more news by then. As well, the Eton's own physician—Dr. Towner, was it?—would have had the opportunity to call in on the patient and add his own evaluation.

Dr. Mesardjian patted the back of Bella's hand. He mustered up a reassuring smile. He advised her to get her beauty sleep and reassured her that the hospital staff would call if there were any change in Mr. Eton's condition. He left.

Robert Hutchins took charge. Nell, it was decided, would drive Bella and Henny back to Salem. It was best if she spent the night there. That way, Robert pointed out practically, Nell wouldn't have to make the long drive back to Newburyport in the dark and she could be there if Bella or Henny needed anything. Robert himself would return to Boston.

"But I am only a phone call away," he told the three women. "And I will be at the house early, Bella. Probably before you've finished your beauty sleep, and we'll reconnoiter and get ourselves back here to the hospital. Tice may surprise us. He has before."

"Beauty sleep!" said Bella crossly.

"I'll give you a half a sleeping tablet," Henny promised. "You'll sleep fine.

Darkness enveloped Nell's car as she found her way down Route 114 toward Salem. From the corner of her eye, she saw Bella's head bob with weariness. In the backseat, the usually talkative Henny was silent. Nell parked the car in the courtyard and the women crept into the house through the back door. It was dark and very quiet. Nell wondered if Derek were still there. The murmur of a television somewhere deep in the house suggested where he was, but if Derek heard the women come in, he gave no sign or greeting.

Henny opened the refrigerator.

"Anyone want warm milk?" she asked. "I could heat some. Never could stand the thought of warm milk myself but they're always giving it to folks who've been through stress and need rest."

"No thanks," said Nell. "I agree with you, Henny."

"Not for me," Bella said emphatically. "I wouldn't mind an inch of Drambuie though. That'd knock me out and I want to be knocked out."

Henny set off for the bar in the dining room and with a murmured excuse, Nell took herself off to search for Derek Eton.

The living room was dark. And empty. Nell fumbled her way into the room, found a lamp and switched it on. Then she continued her prowl, making her way up the stairs. The sound of canned laughter guided her to a room lighted only by the cold flicker of a television screen. Sitting on the end of his spine, as he had the evening Nell met him, was Derek Eton.

"I wasn't sure where I'd find you," Nell told him softly.

He turned to look at her. His head moved but the rest of him did not.

"How is he?"

Deciding the inquiry was sufficient invitation, Nell came into the room and sat down.

"Reasonably stable, they say, but still not conscious. Do you mind if we turn that thing off?"

She jerked her head toward the set. Derek gave the request several beats before aiming the remote and lowering the volume. Nell waited, looking at him levelly until he pressed the power-off button. He looked at her, waiting.

"How did you make out this evening?" she asked. "Did you get something to eat? Find everything you needed?"

The young man shrugged. "I made out okay."

His eyes moved to the dead television screen.

"I wonder if you'd mind telling me what happened."

"To Tice?"

"To your great-grandfather, yes."

Another shrug.

"How should I know?"

"You were with him this morning. I thought that's what they said. Did you see anything unusual? Did he seem okay?"

"He seemed fine." Derek's answer was sullen. "We talked. He felt like taking a nap apparently, so I left."

As if a riveting program were playing on the dark TV, he continued to watch the screen. Nell watched him for a while. When Derek didn't move or speak, she sighed and slowly stood.

"I'll say good night then."

"Night," he replied. Eventually.

Nell stepped to the door and Derek Eton pressed the remote.

Chapter 36

Nell was helping Henny DeFelice assemble breakfast when Bella Eton, wearing a wrapper in a becoming shade of shell pink, made her way into the kitchen.

"Sleep well?" Nell said just as Henny was asking "How did you sleep?"

Bella smiled tiredly.

"As well as can be expected. Isn't that the customary phrase? I didn't hear the phone ring during the night."

She looked anxiously at the other two as if half-expecting one or the other would mention that a phone call had come from the hospital. But Nell and Henny shook their heads.

"No news is good news," said Henny.

Arabella, Nell noticed, had dark gray smudges under both eyes—shadows that hadn't been there the day before.

"Coffee's what you need!" said Henny stoutly, filling one of Bella's favorite Wedgewood ivy cups to the brim and handing it to her.

"Let's take our coffee into the sunroom," Bella said. "The

light in there is so cheering. I suppose Dr. Towner will be calling anytime, don't you? They make their rounds early, so I expect we'll hear..."

Her words drifted away. But Henny and Nell were quick to agree that they surely would hear. Could be any minute now, in fact.

But they didn't hear any minute. And the minutes added themselves up one by one as they sat in Bella's chintz-covered chairs in the sunroom.

"If you don't get a call within fifteen minutes, we'll place our own call to Dr. Towner," Nell was telling her consolingly, when Derek, barefooted, walked into the room.

"Coffee smells good," he said.

"Good morning," said Nell crisply

"Oh. Mornin'. Is there any coffee?"

"I'll get you a cup," Henny offered grimly.

"Derek." Arabella was sitting up very straight. "I'd like to ask you a few things about yesterday. You were the last person to see Tice before...well, before the... incident."

Derek accepted the coffee from Henny.

"So? Go ahead."

"I believe you'd gone to Tice's room to talk with him. Is that right?"

"Yeah."

"And what did you talk about? Was he upset?"

"Upset? No. Not 'specially. We just...you know...talked."

Derek took a noisy sip of the coffee.

Henny DeFelice spoke up crisply. "I think you did more than just talk," she told him. "I heard raised voices."

Derek shot her a sharp look.

"You weren't there," he told her.

"No, but I was in the next room making up the bed and I heard you. Talking! My left foot! Raised voices is what I heard.

And they got louder and louder. Both of you! You were arguing, weren't you?"

"What were you fighting about?" Bella leaned forward intently.

Derek gave the all-purpose shrug.

"It was insignificant. I can't even remember."

"Try!" Arabella ordered. "Try to remember and try hard!"

Nell was surprised. She'd never heard Bella sound so sharp. She'd had no idea Bella was capable of such angry imperative.

"Money, if you must know. I simply pointed out to Tice that he could do better things with his dough than he appeared to be doing."

"Like leave more of it to you, young man?"

"Well, we're young enough to put it good use," Derek told her. "Me and Indigo. Mikey and Crystal too, for that matter. I don't see any sense in relics over the age of eighty sitting around like a couple of misers counting their cash when family could be using it constructively."

"And that made him mad," Nell supplied softly.

"Well, yeah," Derek laughed. "I guess he wasn't any too pleased to hear that."

"What did he say to you?" Arabella asked harshly.

"Nothing. He didn't say anything. He started to and then he just stopped. Decided to take a nap instead. Just closed his eyes."

"So what did you do?"

"Do? Nothing. I let him sleep. I didn't disturb him, I just quietly left the room."

Bella's eyes registered horror.

"You left him there? Slumped in his wheelchair like that? He wasn't taking a nap! You surely knew that! He was ill! Tice is old and he is ill. He'd already had one stroke and you just pushed him into another. And you didn't go for help! You left him alone!"

Bella came slowly out of her chair. She set her cup and saucer down on the side table as she rose, but her eyes never once left her great-grandson's face.

Derek shrugged again. This seemed to inflame Bella further.

"And rather than come and tell me, or tell Henny, that he was acting unusual, you shut the door and didn't say one word! Not a single word. Do you know what you are? You're pond scum! Nothing but pond scum!"

This, from the elegant, elderly lady, caught Derek Eton by surprise and he snickered.

"Oooh, that stung!"

The remark infuriated Bella all the more. Her knuckles brushed the side of an Orfors bowl on the table and her fingers flexed.

"You little... you little shit!" she spit.

At this Derek burst out laughing. Still carrying his coffee, he stood and sauntered insolently from the room.

Bella struggled to regain her breath and composure as she continued to glare at the spot where he'd been standing.

"I wanted to hurl the bowl at him," she whispered to Nell and Henny. "I wanted to see it shatter into hundreds of tiny crystal shards around his head. But I stopped myself."

She took in a large breath, then released it slowly. "It would have been a waste of a pretty bowl."

Nell and Henny had been like ice sculptures during the scene, but now they thawed and moved. And quickly. Henny gathered Bella into her arms but before anyone could speak, the doorbell rang. Nell hurried to answer it.

"Oh, Robert," she said weakly. "Thank God it's you!"

"You've heard from the doctor then?" said Robert, leaping

to a logical conclusion.

But Nell shook her head.

"It's Derek. Derek just admitted he got into a blow-out with Tice..."

"And left him for dead," finished Arabella. She had come silently to the door and now stood in the hall in her pink wrapper; her arms hung at her sides. "Left him for dead," she repeated. "Left him there for who-knows-how-long, when everyone knows that fast action after a stroke can go so far toward saving a life."

But Robert wasn't to get the details of this outrage immediately, for the telephone finally did ring, making them all jump. Henny grabbed for it and they heard her say breathlessly, "Yes! Yes, she's right here, Dr. Towner. Just a second, please."

And she thrust the receiver at Bella. The others eavesdropped unabashedly, but the overheard conversation was short and unsatisfying. Arabella hung the phone up gently. She looked at them.

"No change," she said tiredly. "He made it through the night—that's the good news I guess—but he still isn't conscious and the vital signs—whatever they are—haven't stabilized."

Her shoulders sagged, but then she straightened them.

"Joe Towner will see us at the hospital though. He has some other patients to see and he said he'd meet us as soon as we can get there."

Robert once again took charge.

"Get dressed then—and quickly, Bella. I'll drive you over and stay, of course. Henny, you'd better hold down the fort here..."

"I'll call Frank Largent," Henny said quickly. "He has to know and he will be devastated if we keep the news from him a minute longer than necessary."

"And what about me?"

Derek had apparently been standing at the head of the stairs listening to the conversation. He started down the stairs now and Nell registered, ridiculously, that his feet were still bare and his toenails, long and yellow, needed trimming.

"My flight to California takes off at two."

The others stared.

"I'll drive him in," Nell Bane said grimly. "The rest of you do what you have to do. I'll stay here until noon, then take Derek to Logan."

Henny, muttering, headed for the kitchen presumably to see that Bella had a substantial breakfast and to phone Frank Largent. Robert patted Bella's shoulder and sent her upstairs to dress. Derek vanished up the stairs ahead of his great-grandmother, and Robert and Nell were left alone in the hall. Bella paused though and turned to look down at them.

"I've never used language like that in my life," she said.

"Well, you picked an excellent time to start," Nell told her heartily.

Chapter 37

With Derek Eton in the passenger's seat, Nell drove as far the traffic circle in silence. She couldn't think what to say to this awful young man. From time to time she stole sideways glances at him. He sat stoically, looking straight through the windshield. Impossible to read. Maybe he wasn't as unfeeling as he seemed. Perhaps he was horrified at what he had done? Ashamed? She couldn't tell, but her attitude began to soften.

"Who am I to judge?" she asked herself. She broke the silence.

"Which airline?"

"JetBlue."

Silence.

"Well." Nell said, cracking the quiet once more. "You've seen Salem and you've met your great-grandparents. Any impressions?"

She didn't think he was going to answer. He had turned to gaze out of the side window.

"Old," he said. "Old places. Old people."

"That's true," Nell admitted. "Anything wrong with old?"

The shrug. Well, that was to be expected. Nell persevered.

"You had some opportunities for one-on-one conversation with your great-grandfather. What did you two talk about?"

"Oh—politics. Religion."

"Swell," Nell said. "All the classic taboo subjects. How did it happen you omitted sex?"

"Oh, we talked about that too."

Nell rolled her eyes.

"So, did you learn what some of his views are?"

Nell was surprised that the young man actually seemed to be considering the question.

"Yeah. I learned he was a fossil. Stubborn as mud. And I found out he is a capitalist."

There was surprise in Derek's voice about this last revelation.

"And why should that be surprising? Money isn't a dirty word, you know. I gathered, from what you said earlier to your great-grandmother, that money is something you'd like to have more of. You seem to have the feeling that your great-grandparents should have released a good deal more of it to your parents and to you and your sister as well."

Derek made a sound that Nell couldn't interpret. She shot him a sharp look. He didn't elaborate, though, so she went on.

"Prentice and Arabella Eton came from families that were in comfortable circumstances, and they inherited family money that had been saved and invested and spent wisely. They continued to be good stewards of that wealth. Do you know what that means, Derek? Stewardship?"

There was no response, but Nell told herself that he was listening, so she continued.

"It's an ethical concept. It means the responsible management of resources left in one's care. That includes planning and saving and yes, spending—spending wisely. There can be stewardship in any number of things. In the care of personal property. In all types of financial management like banking where institutions and the individuals who run them have fiduciary responsibilities for the wealth of others. There has to be stewardship in the health fields, of course, and in theology most certainly. There are all sorts of disciplines where responsible management of information and resources is at the very navel of thing. You stand to inherit a considerable financial gift from your great-grandparents, Derek, and if and when that gift comes to you, it will be because Prentice and Arabella have been good stewards. They've cared for what they received and they invested and built on it. They never squandered it. They honored their wealth."

She shot a sideways glance at her passenger and saw his head was turned away from her—turned so he looked out the side window. And still there was no comment. So she took a deep breath and waded on with her homily.

"Part of that stewardship is social responsibility. As you heard, they've given generously to causes they believe are of value to society. These may not be causes you'd espouse, such as the arts or a church, but that's beside the point. They believed in these causes. And this you mustn't forget—you mustn't forget that it is their money."

Nell paused for breath. She'd reached Route 1 and she put another mile on the car's odometer before she opened her mouth again.

"Well! That was quite a sermon. And we're getting close to the airport."

JetBlue flew out of Terminal C so Nell aimed for Logan's central tower. The airport management was continually rearranging routes and logistics, adding signs and upping the speed limits—or so it seemed to Nell—and she had to concentrate as they whizzed toward the tower. She squinted at the icons on the overhead signs even as they squirted beneath them.

Terminal C was within sight, and Nell was concentrating ferociously but she had one more question.

"I have to ask. Do you feel at all culpable for Prentice's condition?"

"Meaning?"

"Meaning responsible. Arguing with him to the extent you did caused a very serious reaction."

"Listen," said Derek. "He's old. He's at the end of his life anyway. I didn't point a gun and shoot him. I merely talked to him. And if he couldn't handle a simple discussion, he shouldn't have participated in it in the first place. I can't be responsible for his reaction when he chose to get involved. So no, I don't feel culpable. When it's time, it's time."

The ubiquitous shrug again. Nell glanced at him.

"I don't expect we'll see each other again," she told Derek, "so I'll say goodbye now. I'll just pull up and drop you off at the curb if that's okay."

"Sure," he mumbled. "G'bye."

And remembering some vestige of manners, added, "Thanks for the ride."

Derek Eton opened the car's back door and pulled out his duffle bag. He headed for the revolving door without a backward glance.

Nell watched him disappear inside the terminal.

Chapter 38

"You're back," Bunty Whitney observed. Nell straightened up slowly from pulling weeds in the border garden and regarded her back-door neighbor.

"Yes," she admitted. "Finally. And I must say this place has gone to hell in a hand-basket since I left Sunday morning."

Bunty peered into Nell's weed bucket.

"Are those deadly nightshades? Don't you hate those? They come up in colonies."

"Like sorrows," Nell agreed. "They come not in spies but in battalions."

"What? Deadly nightshades?"

"Deadly nightshades and sorrows," Nell replied. "There've been plenty of both lately."

"Oh."

Bunty appeared to be meditating on the harvested weeds, and Nell reached down to yank out another fistful of the odious plant.

"And speaking of sorrows, how is Prentice?" Bunty asked.

"Still unconscious."

"That's not good is it?"

"No. The longer he remains that way, the more grave the situation becomes. He's still hanging on though. Robert and Bella are at the hospital almost all the time, taking turns sitting at his bedside."

"Are you off duty then?"

"Not exactly. I spent Sunday night with Bella in Salem, as you know, but everything depends on something else. I want to be available for Bella and be able to relieve Robert. So I expect I'll be looking in at the hospital as long as Tice is there, and if Bella needs someone to stay at night, I'll be in Salem. I stopped into Lahey on my way back from the airport to report that I'd delivered Derek safely into the arms of JetBlue. I was glad to see the backside of that young man, I can tell you."

But that remark further aroused Bunty Whitney's insatiable curiosity.

Nell picked up her bucket of weeds.

"Let me wash my hands and scrape the dirt from under my nails and I'll tell you the whole story. Have you had lunch? I'm chilling a bowl of cucumber and yogurt soup."

So Nell dished up two servings of chilled soup and told Bunty all about Derek Eton as they ate. Bunty's nostrils flared with anger when Nell told her how Derek had argued with Tice, then walked out of the room leaving the old man slumped in his wheelchair.

"Walked out, closed the door, and didn't tell a soul there was a problem."

Bunty was incensed. Always ready to put up her fists on behalf of a wronged party, Derek's action infuriated her and she sputtered righteously.

"Bella confronted him though," Nell told her. "She stood right up to him. Called him a little shit."

"Bella did?" Bunty was delighted. "Terrific. I would have loved to hear that. Did he apologize?"

"Apologize? He laughed! Laughed right in her face! Bunty, how can anyone behave like that?"

Bunty put down her dukes and grew thoughtful. Nell saw the potter recede as the former psychotherapist began to emerge.

"It's an issue of boundaries, I think," Bunty said. "He can't truly distinguish between his needs and his wants. Moreover, he can't—or won't—distinguish between them. All he sees is what someone else has that might meet those needs-slash-wants. What's mine is mine and what's yours is mine."

Nell grunted in agreement.

"He's been brought up to feel entitled, I imagine," Bunty said. "Probably been given everything he's asked for by overly permissive parents—parents who were themselves raised without boundaries. You haven't met the parents have you?"

Nell shook her head.

"It'd be my guess," continued Bunty, "that the parents have told the kiddies that the Etons have more money than God. The kids have probably long resented not getting handsome handouts. So the entitlement may be set in two generations. You know what they say about welfare—after three generations it is a way of life. Immutable."

"But Bunty," Nell couldn't let this go, "how can Derek stand there and deny what's happened? He simply won't acknowledge his responsibility. I never heard of such a thing!"

"Sure you have," Bunty said softly. "You hear about it on the news every week. Hit and run. Someone hits a pedestrian and leaves them dead in the roadway. Doesn't stop or call for help. Runs. Tries to get away. In other words, tries to deny the whole accident."

Nell raised her eyebrows and could find no fault with

Bunty's argument.

"Denial," Bunty continued, "is one of the most primitive of all defenses. 'I didn't do it. This never happened.' But if denial is the first defense, the second is projection. 'I didn't do it—someone else did it. And they did it to me.' His attitude may be cloaked in arrogance and that may be why you don't easily see what's happening. But wouldn't you say young Derek Eton is using both these primitive defenses?"

Nell nodded reluctantly. But she was loath to let Derek so easily off the hook.

"I simply can't say oh well then, the dear boy is just acting out of his primitive instincts, therefore his actions are acceptable."

"Acceptable," said Bunty, "no, certainly not. But forgivable? Well, that's for you to decide."

"Well, he's back in California now," Nell said. "Good luck to him."

"Bad luck to him, might be a better statement," Bunty grunted.

And Nell saw that the psychotherapist had faded and her beloved, call-a-spade-a-spade neighbor was back.

CUCUMBER AND YOGURT SOUP
1 large cucumber
1 small onion, chopped
1 Tbl olive oil
1-1/2 cups chicken stock
Grated peel and juice of one lemon
1 Tbl fresh dill, chopped
1 cup plus 2 Tbl plain yogurt
Salt and pepper to taste
Fresh dill sprigs for garnish
Nell reserved two inches of unpeeled cucumber and

chopped the rest. In a large saucepan, she sautéed the onion in the olive oil, and when it was soft, added the cucumber, the stock, the lemon peel and juice and the chopped dill.

She brought this to a boil, then simmered it covered for 20 minutes. She pureed the mixture with her immersion blender and poured it into a bowl to cool in the refrigerator. When it was cold, she stirred in the yogurt.

When Bunty was comfortably settled at the kitchen table, Nell seasoned the soup with salt and pepper and thinly sliced the reserved cucumber and floated it on the soup's surface, then garnished the bowls with the reserved yogurt and the chopped dill.

Chapter 39

The days and nights snailed by and in the first forty-eight hours after Tice's stroke, the days and nights became almost indistinguishable from one another. Nell made trips to Lahey each day to check on Robert and Bella who were there well into most evenings. When she could pry one or the other away, she took them across the acre of pavement that separated the hospital from the shopping mall and attempted to get a proper meal into them at Legal Seafoods.

She became proficient at finding the ICU waiting room and grew quite good at giving directions when she found others blundering helplessly through the hospital's maze of corridors. Relatives of other ICU patients arrived in the waiting room, introduced themselves, stayed for a short time, and left as their loved ones graduated to other floors. Goodbyes were said and well-wishes bestowed every day, but Prentice Eton did not graduate and Robert Hutchins, Arabella and Nell remained in the waiting room. Veterans of the wait. Ben Wallace, the Etons' minister, often called in to sit with them quietly and his presence seemed to comfort Bella.

Frank Largent, not entirely recovered from bronchitis, slipped the surly bonds of the sister in Quincy and moved back into his apartment over the Eton carriage house. He was very clear about it. Bella and Henny needed a man on premises. Horrifying bouts of coughing coming from the carriage house at all hours made Henny shudder.

Then came the news that Tice was growing weaker. His vital signs were flagging. His breathing was becoming labored and it appeared his kidneys were shutting down.

Robert drew Nell into the corridor and broke this news gently.

"Oh, Robert. How is Bella taking this?"

"As you'd imagine she would. Stoically. She doesn't want to leave his side. I've persuaded her that she can't do this round the clock, so we've worked out a shift arrangement. One of us stays on watch while the other naps on a cot in a family room the hospital has."

"I can spell you too," Nell was quick to offer. "You both need your rest."

"Thank you," said Robert simply. "We'll see. We may have to call on you."

But as it happened, that was unnecessary. The call never came. That very night Prentice Eton slid out of his life at three A.M. Robert Hutchins was at his bedside and reached over to lovingly caress the old man's forehead in a physical benediction.

Bella Eton was devastated to have been in the next room sleeping when he died, but she was a practical woman.

"He wasn't alone, Robert," she said. "That's what's important. You were with him and you were as close as any son. When George left us, you were all the son he had and he loved you dearly. I'm glad you were with him."

"I think, Bella," Robert said, "that Prentice wanted it that way. He waited until you were safely asleep to slip away. He cared for you so much and he protected you right to the end."

Chapter 40

The days that followed felt hollow but they were busy days too. And Nell found she could be of help in the house on North Federal Square. The phone and doorbell rang incessantly. People called with condolences and questions, and a constant procession of flowers and cakes arrived at the door. Henny kept brewing great pots of tea and arranging plates of cookies as the Etons' closest friends stopped by to see Bella. ("Just stopped for a few minutes, dear." "Needed to see how you are holding up." "So, so sorry, Arabella.")

There were people to notify and obituaries to write. Nell found she could be very helpful with these. Ben Wallace sat with Arabella to go over the plans that Tice had specified for his memorial service and to add touches that Bella wished. The service, they agreed, should be held two weeks later.

"The Grands and Greats need time to make their arrangements," Bella said pragmatically. "We can't expect Michael's family to up-sticks and fly all the way from San Franciso on a moment's notice. And Martha will be coming from Atlanta and Brittany from Chicago. No. We'll push this service out a-ways. Give everybody's emotions the opportunity to calm down some too."

Robert got in touch with Martha Baker and Nell called Brittany. Robert talked with Michael and made reservations for the Californians to stay at the Hawthorne Inn across the Common, although Martha and Brittany were going to be billeted in the family house.

"I think Michael's family will be more comfortable at a little remove from this house," Bella said tactfully. "They'll have more privacy at the Hawthorne. More space."

Privately, Nell wondered how the California Etons—especially Derek—felt about this event. Were Michael and Crystal aware of the part their son had played in Prentice's demise? What did Derek think about returning to Salem so soon after leaving in disgrace? On the other hand, did he even realize he was in disgrace? Bunty had explained to Nell that people did not always recognize their wrongdoings. Or if they did recognize them, they often found the guilt so oppressive that it was necessary to shove the responsibility away from themselves. Project it out onto someone else. In this case, Derek was blaming Tice for bringing on the fatal stroke. Hadn't he said as much to Nell?

"If the old man couldn't handle the emotion of the argument, he shouldn't have participated in it."

Nell's blood still boiled when she thought of Derek sitting there in her very car and saying that! Saying it cool as you please. Accountability. He had none.

And she remembered what she'd said to him at the very end of the ride, just three weeks ago.

"I don't expect we'll see each other again," she'd said.

Well, now they were going to see each other and Nell wasn't sure she could be civil. It all depended on Derek. If he could act contrite...if he could grieve for his great-grandfather, well then, she might be mollified.

But it was all speculation. On the day of Prentice's memorial service—the day they'd all be sitting in South Union Congregational Church—well, that day would come soon enough, and then they'd see.

Chapter 41

Accompanied by Jerry Gasso, Nell stepped into the third pew and seated herself next to Frank Largent. Henny DeFelice leaned around Frank's bulk to nod at Nell, then fished a tissue out of her handbag and wiped her nose. They waited. The organ mumbled. Nell caught a snatch of *Sheep May Safely Graze.* Someone behind them coughed. Cellophane crinkled as the cougher unwrapped a hard candy. The silence was resumed.

On a table at the front of the church, was a handsome mahogany box in which, Nell assumed, reposed the ashes but not the soul of the late Prentice Eton. It had been centered between a pair of casual flower arrangements. Small sunflowers, deep blue cornflowers, golden rod, Queen Anne's Lace, loosestrife and Joe Pye—the field flowers of August. Nell smiled her approval.

The organ maundered into something Purcell and down the aisle paced the Eton family. Arabella, straight-backed and with one gloved hand resting on the arm of Robert Hutchins, led the procession. They paused at the front, waiting while

Bella gazed at the mahogany cask. Then, with the precision of a jeweler setting a precious stone, Robert seated Arabella in the front pew. The rest of the family—the Grands and Greats—dithered in the aisle for a moment until Brittany Baker, looking perfectly composed, took the initiative and stepped into the pew behind her great-grandmother. She was followed by an older woman whom Nell took to be her mother, Martha Baker. Harmon Baker, the much-absent husband and father, was not with them. Brittany's pregnancy was very evident and the lovely blue dress she had chosen accentuated her condition.

Now Michael Eton tried to organize his family. He indicated that his wife was to proceed into the pew after the Baker women. She did so, leading a stumbling Indigo by the wrist. Indigo's face was blotchy and swollen and her eyes were pink from weeping. She looked close to collapse. Her hair, however, was still violently blue. Michael Eton stepped into the pew and gestured for his son to take the aisle seat. Derek Eton, dropping into the pew, managed to give the impression of extreme fatigue. Or extreme boredom.

The Reverend Dr. Benjamin Wallace stepped to the front of the church.

"Good morning."

Ben Wallace paused to smile and look around at the congregation. His gaze rested for a few moments on Bella Eton and his smile became tender.

"And as we gather here to celebrate the life of Prentice Eton, it is a good morning, for we are remembering and honoring a good man. An exceptional man. So let us draw near to God this morning and remember before him his servant Prentice Eton."

There was a responsive call to worship, and when the congregation had waded through it, Dr. Wallace continued.

"One of Prentice's favorite hymns was *God Of Our Fathers.*

It has a fine military sound that touched his patriotism, but this hymn also says a great deal about the man himself. About his values. And especially about his feelings for family and those ancestors who came before him. He always stood very tall when he sang it and this morning I'd like to hear you sing it out loud. Sing the way he would have. Sing it especially for Prentice."

Dr. Wallace nodded at the organist who set the trumpet stops to deliver a triumphant heralding, and the congregation—with scuffling feet, rustling hymnals and preparatory coughs and throat clearings— struggled to its feet.

God of our fathers whose Almighty hand / Leads forth in beauty all the starry band.

Jerry Gasso—Nell had never realized this—had a fine tenor voice. Jerry sang the challenging tenor line with assurance as it moved against the melody. Nell was impressed. On her other side, Frank Largent rumbled a bronchial bass that made up for in depth what it lacked in tunefulness. From the pew ahead, Nell caught snatches of Brittany Baker's clear soprano. She held the hymnal for her mother but looked straight ahead as she sang, glancing down only occasionally for cues to the lyrics. The enthusiastic singing encouraged Nell to add her halting alto to the mix. She had a shy enjoyment of singing and— when supported by heartier voices—could feel very inspired indeed.

Thy love divine hath led us in the past / In this free land by Thee our lot is cast; / Be Thou our ruler, our guardian, guide and stay, / Thy word our law, Thy paths our chosen way.

The organist pulled a stop that sent the trumpet a half-tone higher and a chill went up Nell's neck. Michael Eton's family looked bemused. Crystal made no attempt to sing. Indigo swayed woozily against her mother, obviously suffering too much grief to give way to music. Michael held an open hymnal and gazed at it as if he'd never seen one before, and Derek stood with one hand in his pocket, surveying the ceiling.

From war's alarms, from deadly pestilence / Be Thy strong arm our ever sure defense...

The organ shifted again, preparing to bring out the final stanza in a blaze of trumpets and glory.

Refresh thy people on their toilsome way / Lead us from night to never-ending day...

An air of satisfaction hung over the congregation as the hymn wound down into ... *And praise be ever-ver Thine.*

As the hymn ended, the congregation was treated to one final trumpet blast. Frank Largent, overcome with emotion, blew his nose into a large white handkerchief.

"That was wonderful," he whispered fervently to Nell. "Just beautiful!"

Ben Wallace smiled. "I think that was splendid. Prentice would be very pleased. Now let's come together in prayer."

Heads obediently bowed.

"Gracious Spirit, Creator of Life and Carrier of Hope, make your presence known to us this day. Help us to be brave in our suffering, honest in our sorrow and open to one another in remembering. Help us to remember with joy the life of Prentice Eton, whom we have loved and who we remember today, knowing that your love will not let us go and will never let us down. Grant us your peace."

Amens mumbled through the congregation at the close of the prayer and Dr. Wallace addressed them once more.

"And now, Robert Hutchins, a dear and long-time friend of the Etons', will offer some words of remembrance."

Robert Hutchins stood, but as ever, his good manners preceded him and he took a moment to turn to Bella with a special smile and a touch on her shoulder before stepping up to the podium.

"Where are his notes?" Nell breathed to Jerry Gasso.

"He never uses them," Jerry whispered back. "He works without a net. More dangerous. Robert is mad for danger."

Jerry grinned.

Robert paused. And he drew out the pause just long enough to seed a thin wedge of tension within the congregation. Just long enough to make a few of the more sensitive souls wonder if he would be alright. Then suddenly he looked up and smiled wonderfully.

"Prentice Eton was a wealthy man but he didn't perceive the wealth as entirely his. Rather he saw himself as a custodian of funds—his temporarily to be used for the good. He took it as his duty to increase the wealth and to pass it on. This role—this charge—was deeded to him from his father and before that, from his grandfather and from their fathers before them. It was a responsibility, and Tice carried it without flagging or complaining.

"Prentice also counted his wealth in other ways: In his good fortune to marry the beautiful Arabella Whiteside, his wife of more than sixty years. He counted it in his children, Caroline and George, both of whom—sadly—passed from this life far too soon. And he counted it in his grandchildren and great-grandchildren in whom he perceived the promise of the future. While geography prevented Tice and Bella from seeing as much of their grandchildren and great-grandchildren as they would have liked, they followed their family's affairs and welfare from a distance, loved them and remembered them. Tice was clear that he counted his wealth in family.

"Yes, and he counted it in friends. He was well known and well loved in Salem. Generous to cultural endeavors, to civic and social interests and to his church—this church, South Union—that comforts us today. Tice and Bella were dear friends of my late parents, and I knew them literally from my cradle days. I grew up with George and Caroline and today I stand in the place that is rightly theirs—the place where a child stands when a parent passes away. And I am saying what they might say if they could be here. We have lost a father. A guiding light. An example and role model. A man we dearly loved and love. A man we'll remember."

Robert Hutchins bowed his dark head for a few moments, then looked out clearly at the congregation and nodded before he stepped down.

"Thank you, Robert," said Ben Wallace. "You've helped make Prentice live again for us today. And now, let's come together in silent meditation as we listen to the beautiful music of Mozart.

The organist drifted reverently into *Ave Verum Corpus* and Nell, bowing her head, felt her eyes grow wet. The great music worked its usual transformation, transporting people from the exultation of the opening hymn and the personal reflections of Robert Hutchins's eulogy into a deeper, more sober and reflective place.

Dr. Wallace gave the congregation several minutes to adjust to the present time and place before he invited them softly to receive the words of comfort by joining in the Twenty-third psalm. The congregation murmured the ancient words, familiar to some and perhaps foreign to others. But Nell heard Arabella clearly affirm the last lines in the King James translation: "*Surely goodness and mercy shall follow me all the days of my life and I shall dwell in the house of the Lord forever. Amen.*"

Ben Wallace read the Words of Assurance from John 14. He invited them to share in the Prayer of Remembrance. "Eternal God, behind the sacred mystery of life and death and everlasting life, there is the beating of Your glorious love..."

In the midst of this prayer, Indigo Eton was heard to draw

a long, loud, quavering breath before blurting into a blubber of sobs and snorkels. Crystal threw an arm around her daughter, hugging her close, but Michael Eton looked down at the girl as if he couldn't imagine who this unsavory child might possibly be.

Dr. Wallace continued calmly over the storm and spoke the Amen. Then he smiled reassuringly.

"Grief is difficult," he acknowledged. "Sometimes it is no more controllable than hiccups. It can wash over us—can feel like it is going to wash us away. And that's alright. That's the way life is. Ecclesiastes reminds us that there is a time to mourn and a time to grieve. But there is also a time to dance. A time to lift up our voices in thanksgiving and praise. And so in closing, I ask you to join in singing our closing hymn—another of Prentice's great favorites—*Faith of Our Fathers*."

Again the organ surged and Nell was on her feet once more.

"Faith of our fathers, living still in spite of dungeon, fire and sword," sang Nell, feeling the music rise through her body— feeling it buoy her up like some musical injection of helium and consolation. *"And teach me too,"* she sang, *"as Love knows how / By kindly words and virtuous life."*

That's Tice, she thought as she sang. Kindly words and a virtuous life. A life informed by love. Her mind was flashing on the scenes she'd written in the memoir...Tice in that hot church with the buzzing bluebottle the day of Willard's funeral...Tice saying goodbye to Bella before going off to join Old Blood and Guts Patton and to defend his country against Fascism...Tice, still recovering from war wounds, manfully shouldering the family business in the wake of his father's death and seeking to use the monies he'd earned and inherited in the best ways possible...Tice loving Arabella...loving his children...loving his elders—those who sat at his table and those who were taking their places there no longer.

Then Benjamin Wallace was spreading his robed arms like wings.

"Now may the love of God abide with you and within you. May it comfort you, guide you, uphold you and sustain you, today and for all the days that are yet to be. May it bring you peace. Amen."

He stepped down from the chancel and bent to Arabella in the first pew. He spoke a few unheard words meant just for her. He left a kiss on her cheek. For Robert Hutchins, there was a warm handshake and some soft words, then with a whisper of robe, he moved swiftly up the aisle.

It was left to the men from Armbruster Funeral Home then, to organize the recessional, and Bella and Robert, arm in arm, were the first to leave. An Armbruster man stood by the second pew to indicate its occupants should rise. Brittany Baker was already standing. And frowning. But Derek Eton, seated on the aisle, seemed not to know what the Armbruster man wanted. Still sprawled in the pew, he looked up at the fellow blankly. Michael nudged him sharply and Derek finally got it. He lurched up and into the aisle like a cork coming out of a bottle, and with the path unplugged, the rest of his family was allowed to file out. Indigo lurched up the aisle in a swoon. Her eyes so swollen from weeping that Crystal was forced to half-carry the girl.

Brittany Baker, still composed but with signs that a tear or two had been shed, moved at a dignified pace beside her mother. Her dress was a perfect summer blue shot with delicate sprays of white flowers. Her glossy hair was caught in a demure twist at the nape of her neck. Her face was serene. Radiant. Martha Baker was still a young woman, Nell saw, but she appeared fragile and dependent upon her daughter.

Now it was Nell's turn. Jerry stepped into the aisle and

turned to allow her to precede him. Frank Largent and Henny DeFelice stepped out also. As she walked up the aisle, Nell recognized a number of faces. There was an impressive contingent from the Peabody Essex Museum, including the people Nell had met at the book signing party. Friends from the Symphony, from South Union, even from the neighborhood stood in their places in the pews, waiting respectfully for the close family and relatives to pass. Bunty Whitney had driven down from Newburyport and she caught Nell's eye. Nell recognized faces she knew from the past few weeks—people who had stopped by the house with condolences and cheer, with spiral-cut hams and macaroni casseroles. The church was full. And they were all there to pay tribute to a man much loved and respected. Nell wondered what—if anything—young Derek Eton made of this show of affection.

At the front doors of the church, people milled a bit and sought out friends. Nell found Bunty.

"Are you coming to the collation back at the house?" she asked. "Bella would love to see you."

But Bunty had to get back to Newburyport.

"Tell Bella I'll stop in during the next week or so. Give her my compliments on a beautiful service. And give her my love."

Chapter 42

Bella had hired a fleet of caterers to produce a collation for the mourners who would stop back to the house after the memorial service. As well, half dozen ladies from Bella's church circle surged into the kitchen as supplemental troops and were soon jostling with the professional team. Henny tried to get involved and was promptly shooed from the kitchen by a couple of church ladies. Her apron was untied and she was told to get herself into the more public rooms of the house. There were people out there wanting to speak to her.

Bella stood before the fireplace in the living room, receiving guests and condolences. Robert Hutchins finally made her sit in a chair and assured her that it was quite correct, under the circumstances, to greet people in a seated position. Everyone would understand.

Nell drifted to a window seat where Crystal Eton sat with Indigo. Nell greeted Indigo and introduced herself to Michael's wife. Crystal might once have been a lovely Flower Child but her season had passed, and now she was just an overblown posy with lank hair and a couple inches of flesh rolling over her waistband.

"That was a very moving service, I thought," Nell said. "Are you recovered, Indigo?"

The girl was balancing a plate of pastries and she looked up, her mouth stuffed with most of a cannoli. She licked cannoli off her fingers and with a full mouth, indicated with vigorous nods that she was better.

Her mother spoke up for her.

"Poor Indigo was just devastated! She adored her great-grandfather, you know. And this is her first experience with death. Her very first funeral and the first time she's lost someone near and dear."

Nell was surprised that Indigo and Tice had been so close, but she made sympathetic sounds and nodded her head.

Indigo swallowed the last of the cannoli, selected a petit choux and bit into it. Custard erupted from both sides of the puff.

"I guess that's why the Brits call them gooeys," Nell smiled. "Well, I hope you have a safe trip home to California. San Francisco is it? Or San Diego. I'm sorry, I can't remember."

And having been told it was San Fran, Nell moved on through the crowd, speaking to those she knew slightly and nodding to others, but the rooms were thick with people she did not know. She saw Jerry Gasso in animated conversation with a couple she didn't recognize. She looked for Derek Eton, but did not spot him. Moreover, the house was beginning to overheat. Nell went through the kitchen and slipped out the back door.

The garden was small but lovely. A gravel path that traced an oval was lined with boxwood that Frank Largent kept fastidiously clipped. In the oval's center a three-tiered fountain spilled water from a vessel hefted by a sturdy bronze woman whose gown was slipping off one shoulder in the Greek style. The sound of splashing water was welcome on the hot day. Nell took a deep breath of the still August air and exhaled.

"You're escaping too," said a voice. Brittany Baker was sitting on a stone bench sipping ice water. "I thought I would pass out in there," she said. "How is Bella holding up?"

"She's remarkable. Would you mind some company or is this a private party?" Nell said.

Brittany moved down the bench to make room.

"I expect she's being carried along on adrenalin," Nell continued, "but at some point she'll crash from exhaustion— and she deserves to. It's been a grueling month. First all the trauma of Tice's stroke, then the grief of his death and finally the planning for the memorial service. That's quite a marathon for anyone to run."

She changed the subject.

"Had you met your California cousins before today?"

"No. And I barely met them today. They're rather clannish and they don't seem inclined to mingle."

Nell decided no comment was called for, so she simply nodded. Brittany took a sip of ice water.

"Can I ask you something? I heard something disturbing. I heard that Derek was with Tice when he had the stroke. And he did nothing to save him. Just walked out of the room and closed the door. Is that so?"

"Mind telling me where you heard it?"

"In the kitchen. I came down early and had breakfast with Henny and Frank. They are extremely upset. Didn't pull any punches."

Nell nodded. "They wouldn't."

"And Frank was blaming himself. Excoriating himself up and down for the whole thing. Said if he'd been here, Tice wouldn't have been alone. If he'd only been here none of this would have happened."

"Oh dear. The poor man. I'll have a word later. You know it's a funny thing, Brittany. There are people who are so quick to wrap themselves in guilt and responsibility. Ready to cry *mea culpa* when they aren't even culpable. And then there are those who should be beating their breasts and hanging their heads in shame, and they just go blandly on claiming innocence."

"Like Derek, you mean."

"Well, I didn't say that."

A corner of Brittany's mouth tucked into an ironic smile.

"And I never heard it."

She watched the water splashing for several moments.

"My mother's flying back to Atlanta tomorrow, but I asked Bella if I could stay for a few days. I'd like the chance to be with her after all the commotion settles down. I know she'll be exhausted but perhaps a bit of quiet company would ease her into her new situation. You know, so busy-busy one day and the next absolutely nothing."

"I think that's a wonderful idea," Nell said warmly. "Very perceptive of you. And how are you, by the way? You're looking radiant."

"Pretty well, considering," the young woman replied. "It's been a fairly easy pregnancy up to now and I've been able to work. Now I can count the weeks to the birth in single digits."

"And after? You have your plans made?"

"Maternity leave, of course, but yes, the nursery is ready, baby care is arranged. Just have to pack a suitcase."

"Boy or girl? Do you know?"

Brittany shook her head.

"I like the element of surprise."

The two women sat in companionable silence, feeling the heat of the day on their faces and being grateful for the light spray from the fountain that an occasional breeze misted their way.

Nell sighed and slapped her hands on her thighs.

"Well I guess I can't hide out here forever. Better get back in there and make one more round before I say my goodbyes."

"The crowd is thinning out," Brittany observed. "I think you'll be fine."

And Brittany was right. The guests were leaving or preparing to leave, and Nell at last found Jerry Gasso and then Robert Hutchins and finally Bella Eton, and gave her farewells. But descending the granite steps she glanced across the Common and spotted a familiar figure standing under a tree and gazing up at the house with the air of a prospective buyer contemplating a purchase. Their eyes met and Nell started to cross North Federal Square to speak to the young man. But Derek shoved his hands in his pockets, made a rapid about-face and walked off briskly across the Common toward the Hawthorne Inn. Nell, brought up short, watched him go. Then he stopped. Stopped with a slight jerk, the way a dog stops when its leash is suddenly yanked. Nell watched as he turned slowly and faced her. Derek drew his hands out of his pocket as he approached her.

Nell waited. Derek was scowling.

"Do you remember what you said to me when you dropped me off at the airport? Do you?"

Nell regarded him calmly.

"Not chapter and verse, no. What exactly are you referring to?"

"That part about probably never seeing each other again. Do you remember that? Well here we are again, face to face."

And Derek pushed his face so close to Nell's that two fists could barely have passed between them. She didn't flinch.

"I do remember that," she said, still calm. "Why? What's

your point?"

Derek backed off with a loud exhale. Perhaps he'd meant to intimidate her—thought he could—and then seen the bluff hadn't worked. The exhale appeared to deflate him.

"Nothing," he mumbled. "Just wondered is all."

He turned again to leave. Nell spoke up clearly.

"I'm sorry about your great-grandfather. I'm sure it's difficult to lose a close relative under any circumstances. I'm sorry for your loss. But are you sorry—sorry at all—for your failure to call an ambulance or to call Bella or at the very least, to have turned back yourself to check on him?"

There it was again—the Derek shrug.

"I'm sorry he's dead. I'm sorry he had the stroke, I suppose. But he brought it on himself. I didn't do it. I don't see how anyone can blame me."

His sentence ended in a whine and Nell was disgusted.

"No, I don't suppose you can see how," she said.

"Everyone has a lecture to give," Derek sneered. "Tice. Bella. You!"

Nell saw his hands clench into fists.

"Thanks for driving me to the airport," he said sarcastically, "but you lectured me all the way and you're still harping on that same old note."

And this time Derek did not turn back once he stalked off across the Common. Nell watched him all the way until he reached the Inn's doors and disappeared.

Chapter 43

There is no such thing as bad weather, only bad clothing. And Nell, outfitted in GoreTex and Mudruckers, was dry and comfortable as she walked on the beach. A seasonal hurricane had come up the coast, scrutinized and reported on rapaciously by New England weather broadcasters.

"A named storm," they had crowed, "with winds up to eighty miles-per-hour, is headed for New England and expected to make a direct hit!"

Nell thought they sounded joyful. The television ratings would be rising in direct relation to the barometer's fall. But the named storm expended most of its energy over the Carolinas, which, Nell reflected, must have been very disappointing to the weather media. Still, a residual nor'easter was blowing in abnormally high tides and there were gusty winds and smatterings of rain. Not enough to keep Nell inside though, and she was enjoying the solitude of the beach, the light rain and salt spray on her face and the fresh wind that she imagined was blowing out the old and bringing in the new.

A great deal had happened since Robert Hutchins had introduced her to Prentice and Arabella Eton. Not so much in terms of time—for in the tight space of ten months, she had learned the couple's stories and woven them into a memoir—an accounting of two splendid lives. As well, Nell had made two new friends. Actually more, if you counted Henny DeFelice and Frank Largent. Oh, and Brittany Baker. Nell had grown fond of the Etons' great-granddaughter. Pity she couldn't say the same of Indigo and Derek.

But now it was time for fresh woods and pastures new. And thanks to the Etons' generosity, Nell could afford to be patient about waiting for the next ghostwriting assignment.

She wondered what it would be and from which quarter it would blow.

It had been nearly two weeks since Prentice Eton had been memorialized, his ashes interred, and the caterers packed up and gone from North Federal Square. Quiet and calm had been restored to the house, according to Henny. Even Brittany Baker had kissed them all goodbye and returned to Chicago. Nell had spoken briefly to Bella and at some length to Henny but it was time to give them some peace.

Into this interlude, Madeline Kaiser called with an invitation to spend five days on Nantucket. Nell was delighted to finally be able to say yes to such a tempting invitation. She happily told Madeline that she was free as swallow on the spring air—or in this case as a seagull over Nantucket Sound—and that she would love to spend time with Madeline on the Island. She'd made it back from the Cape just as the weather gremlins had set up their chatter about the tropical storm.

So Nell had battened down the hatches, settled down to give the house a good cleaning and had made a huge batch of chicken stock. Containers of it were stacked in the freezer ready to be the base of the soup recipes for fall and winter.

NELL'S CHICKEN STOCK
3 carrots, cut into thirds
2 stalks of celery, cut into thirds
1 bulb of fennel, cut into large chunks
3 tablespoons of fennel seeds, toasted
1 teaspoon whole black peppercorns
1 whole chicken, 4 to 6 pounds
2 pounds chicken wings, necks and backs
3 quarts low sodium chicken broth 2 quarts cold water

Nell flung the entire list of ingredients into her stockpot and clapped on the lid. Then, when the mixture reached the boil, she reduced the heat and let the soup simmer, uncovered, for an hour. From time to time she checked to be sure the liquid was barely bubbling and skimmed the surface when foam, looking dirty as brook water, collected at the edges of the pot.

An hour into the process, Nell fished out the whole chicken and dumped it in a large bowl to cool. When there was no danger of burned fingers, she pulled the meat from the bones and put it aside for another day. Back into the pot went the bones. Nell placed a smaller pot lid inside the stockpot to keep the bones submerged, then returned the stockpot to the Aga to simmer for four more hours. The little house took on the fragrance of simmering chicken soup.

Nell prepared an ice bath in a dishpan. She strained the stock through a fine sieve into a large, heatproof bowl which she set in the ice bath. She stirred it often while the stock cooled, it to room temperature. Ah, at last. Nell ladled the stock into stackable freezer containers. With satisfaction, she surveyed her finished work. To seal in the flavors, she'd left a layer of chicken fat on the top of each container, all neatly capped and stored. And she had earned the right to be complacent; to feel provident.

Chapter 44

"Well, this is a pleasant surprise," Nell said when she answered the phone. "I'm so pleased to hear from you! And I must say you sound very chipper."

Nell was having coffee with Bunty Whitney when the call came through and Bunty looked up with interest.

"Who?" she mouthed.

"Bella," Nell mouthed back.

At this Bunty put her chin on her fist and set herself to eavesdrop shamelessly.

"I feel quite chipper," Bella said. "Now Nell, I've made two very important decisions. There's nothing quite so freeing as having made decisions and plotted a course of action, don't you agree?"

Nell did.

"I am curious Bella. Do you plan to let me on these decisions?"

"Certainly, because the first one involves you. Nell, I want to write a new chapter in the book."

Nell was thunderstruck but Bella sailed right on.

"There is something I need to set right. I believe you and Robert told me that this book is what you call print-on-demand. And I was also given to understand that it could be changed at any time and new copies could be ordered. Is that still correct?"

"It is Bella, but I am mystified. What could you possibly want to add now?"

"That is what I want to discuss, my dear, but first I needed to see if you would agree to take on more work. I will pay you whatever you ask, of course," she added hastily. "Are you available for hire?"

"Oh Bella, of course, but are you going to tell me more?"

"When I see you, my dear, when I see you. And I hope that will be as soon as possible. I want to make this significant change very quickly. When can you come to Salem?"

"Would this Thursday be too soon?" Nell asked.

"Thursday will be perfect. Oh, Henny will be so pleased. Come in the morning and we'll work through lunch. Well, with that settled..."

"Bella! Wait! What is the second decision you made?"

"The second decision is to see my attorney. John Dockery. See you Thursday, my dear."

Nell said goodbye and flopped back in her chair.

"Well?" Bunty Whitney demanded.

"She wants to change the memoir. Make a significant change, she said. I can't imagine what she means to do."

"Can she do that?" Bunty asked. "Make a change? I mean the book is published, printed, signed and sent to people. Isn't that the end of it?"

"Not if you're doing print-on-demand, which is how Robert set this book up. It's as simple as making the change and uploading the new file to the online printer. Then you just buy the number of copies you want and—presto!"

"Expensive?"

"Strangely, it's very reasonable."

"What is it she wants to do?" Bunty persisted.

"She wouldn't say. I'll have to wait till Thursday to find out. Therefore you'll have to wait too."

"Goody," Bunty said. "I love mysteries."

Chapter 45

It was pleasant to be back in Arabella's beloved sunroom. A tray with coffee service was set on a low table and there were croissants and fig jam. Nell was suddenly hungry. And Bella, as she poured out two cups of coffee, looked serene. Nell wouldn't have guessed that this woman had so recently endured the emotion of a husband's shocking illness and death as well as the behavior of a great-grandson that had been more than careless—had been downright cruel. Nell inquired gently about this.

"I have gotten quite a bit of rest," Bella explained. "I was exhausted by the time the memorial service was over, I'll admit that. But I lay in my bed and had some serious conversations with myself. Arabella, I told myself sternly, you will just have to reinvent yourself. Carry on. You have this house to look after as well as the welfare of Henny and Frank. They're depending on you. And you have loving friends who have stood by you and come to your aid in your time of trouble. You mustn't overlook all you have been given."

Bella stopped relating her self-conversation and gave Nell an intense look.

"And I'm talking about you," she said. "You are one of the friends who has supplied such sustenance. One of the ones who lent me your strength. So I realized I had to carry on, and as I told you on the telephone, my dear, I set myself two important tasks to accomplish—the first one being a revision of *Looking Forward*. There is something I need to set right. I need to rewrite a complete chapter. I need to tell the truth about the war years."

"The truth?" Nell echoed blankly. "Do you mean your story of the war years was not true?"

"Stories," Bella corrected. "There were a number of stories in that chapter, as there were in Tice's. Some of those stories were true. And some were only true as far as they went. It is in the omissions that the dishonesty occurs. I was not forthright and truthful about some very important things that happened in that time. I want to tell the real story now, and I'd like you to rewrite the chapter."

"Do you mean to replace your chapter of the war years with this new material?" Nell asked.

"I'm not sure," Bella admitted slowly. "I'm not sure if I want to replace the original or simply append the new chapter to end of the book. Perhaps I'll leave that decision to you after it is written."

Nell was silent for several minutes. Then she asked an important question.

"But Bella, why? Why now?"

Arabella smiled.

"It was Brittany. It was her honesty. And her bravery. My admiration for her was deeply stirred. But there's more. I couldn't have told this story as long as Prentice was alive. It violates every tenet—every value—he held dear. Knowledge of this would have killed him as surely as that second stroke. If Derek hadn't provoked it, this would have."

Nell took a sip of coffee and set the cup back in the saucer. She bent over and took the tools of her trade out of her bag.

"Well then," she said, switching the Sony recorder to record, "I guess we'd better get started."

Arabella smiled and sat back in her chair.

Chapter 46

The War Years Amended
Setting The Story Straight
Arabella Whiteside Eton

For me, that period we call "the war years" was bitter-sweet. I was in love. I was in love with Prentice Eton and I wanted nothing so much as to be with him and to be Mrs. Prentice Eton. He had asked me to marry him and indeed, we talked of marrying before he went into the service, but reason—I suppose it was reason—prevailed. Tice was concerned that I might be a widow at age twenty. I think my biggest concern was that there wasn't time to plan the wedding of my dreams— a white satin gown with a train and eight bridesmaids. A wedding that involved choosing the invitations at Shreve's and arranging the wedding gifts on organdy-skirted tables in the library at Pinckney Street. Well, I was young and hadn't yet developed the sense of social responsibility.

But I was in love and I wrote letters to Tice every day. Sometimes, if I was feeling especially bereft, I wrote twice a day. And I read his letters until I learned each by heart. He was busy and didn't have time to write everyday and he explained he wouldn't have that much to say even if he did write. But oh, the letters that arrived were read so many times the stationary grew soft as facial tissue. I'd lie on my back on my bed and read them over and over and tears would leak out of the corners of my eyes and roll into my hair, I missed him so.

And I have his letters still. Faded, they are, but they're tied up with pale blue ribbon and kept in a box in my dresser.

When Tice left, I continued to go to classes at Wellesley. I liked college well enough, but it seemed—I don't know—kind of lame after you'd said goodbye to the man you loved and didn't know if that were the last goodbye you'd ever say.

Those were unusual times. Dreadful in some ways and in other ways exciting. People coming and going. Boys you'd known all your life suddenly showing up in uniform and looking very different. Very dashing. Quite romantic. And the train stations and sidewalks so full of servicemen. Navy whites and blues. Army officers in pinks and greens and enlisted men in sandy khaki. And Marines with that bright red stripe on the trousers. Wolf whistles followed you down the streets as trolleys packed with servicemen clattered past. I think every girl must have felt pretty in those war years, all of us in bobby sox and saddle shoes, flirty pleated skirts that didn't cover our knees and soft sweaters in every color of the rainbow. There were dances and parties because someone you knew was always shipping out or coming home on leave. And oh, the sweet agony of being in love with someone who was far away. I'd hear a recording of Doris Day singing *Sentimental Journey* and an almost unbearable pain would cramp my chest. Or I'd be at a Wellesley dance when the band would strike up *In The Mood* or *One O'Clock Jump* and someone I didn't even know would grab my hand and swing me onto the dance floor and hurl me around till I was giddy. Then the very next song would be something sad and dreamy like *Bluebirds Over The White Cliffs of Dover* and my throat would close up and I'd have the blues again.

I wrote to Tice every day. Not long letters, because when you write every day, there's not much news to share, but I'd fill the letters with declarations of how much I missed him and how much I loved him. And, of course, I haunted the mailbox, praying for his letters to come. But Tice was in Europe by this time. We hadn't seen each other for months and months and his letters arrived less and less frequently. Naturally I was worried.

Now the thing is, I've always had a very fertile imagination. And I tried to control it—I really did—but my imagination used to get out of control and go spinning off into all sorts of crazy places, and I'd be hard put to haul it back in line. I had Tice dead in ditches dozens of times. I had him in prisoner of war camps and in field hospitals. I had him in and out of comas. And then, for variety, I started having fantasies about a girl in Belgium. Why Belgium, I don't know, but in my imagination, Tice had met a beautiful Belgian girl—although sometimes she was French and once even Italian. He was bewitched by this woman and had fallen completely out of love with me. That's why his letters had become so infrequent. He didn't care about me anymore.

I lost interest in my classes at Wellesley. They'd all begun to seem pointless anyway. I told myself that I should be doing something noble to help win this bloody war, and I dropped out of Wellesley and started taking secretarial courses at Katherine Gibbs in Boston. I wanted to qualify as a typist like my friend Betsy Galbraith who was living in New York and doing some kind of war work that involved typing. I could see myself in khaki—in a WAC uniform—and clattering away in a typing pool in a war room turning out secret documents that were vital to the Allied effort.

My parents didn't think much of the Katy Gibbs idea but they didn't object too strenuously, so I moved back home, went to typing classes and in the evenings went out with friends who were partying with determined gaiety and plenty of false bravado.

And that's when I met up with Charlie Thurston. Now I'd known Charlie my entire life. The Thurstons had a camp at Squam just down the lake from the Whiteside compound, and Charlie was one of the kids with whom I'd run through the evenings playing games of Hide and Seek. Charlie used to duck my head underwater, hold me down till I thought I'd drown, but it was all in fun.

Charlie was based at the Charlestown Navy Yard, waiting to be sent overseas, and he took me out to dinner at the Parker House and to a couple of dances out at the Totem Pole. It felt good to hold hands again. To laugh with someone you knew and really liked. Charlie bought me drinks—rum and Coke (I shudder to think of that now)—and listened sympathetically while I cried into my beer about Tice and the Belgian maiden. And...well...one thing led to another, and one night in the Parker House, Charlie took a room upstairs. And there was another time at a party somewhere in the Back Bay where everyone was so loud and carrying on that no one noticed when we slipped upstairs to a back bedroom.

Then Charlie shipped out to the Pacific and things grew quiet again. Poor Charlie. He was assigned to a carrier that took a Kamikaze hit just two weeks he'd arrived. He'd only made one bombing run before that hit ended his life. My mother got the news in a letter from Charlie's mother. I remember coming into the sitting room and there she was beside the fire with Mrs. Thurston's letter in her lap and tears in her eyes, and she told me about Charlie. She said that Charlie was gone. And by that time I knew I was pregnant.

You have to understand how life was in those years. Had I told my family about my situation, it would have caused a great scandal. Worse scandal than my mother's Uncle Henry ever caused with his horse race gambling. I would be seen as a fallen woman, the Whiteside family would be disgraced, and if Tice ever did give up the imaginary Belgian woman and return safely to Boston, I was positive he would not want to marry me.

I was terrified. Finally the only thing I could think to do was to take Betsy Galbraith into my confidence. I'd known Betsy as long as I'd known Charlie Thurston, and I hoped she would know what I could do.

Betsy did. She directed me to come down to New York City immediately. She insisted I could get lodgings, as she had, at the Barbizon Hotel for Women and I could also get a typing job like hers. I finished up at Katy Gibbs, and armed with my certificate and the results of my speed tests, I packed a single suitcase and took a train out of South Station.

That wasn't the easiest thing to do in 1943. The trains were overcrowded, usually late and civilians often had to step aside for servicemen who got priority. Eventually I managed to crowd into a New York Central car and I sat on my suitcase all the way to Providence. When I did get a seat, it was next to a young private who'd been up all night and who promptly fell asleep against my shoulder. He drooled on my jacket. In those days everyone smoked and the car stank of cigarettes and the air was layered with blue smoke. Between the smoke, the rocking car and my delicate condition, I began to feel queasy and spent the whole trip to Manhattan fighting nausea and trying to make myself comfortable without waking the drooling private.

It was confusing and difficult getting from Pennsylvania Station up to the Barbizon on 63rd and Lexington. Everybody pushing and hurrying. And by the time my suitcase and I got to the lobby I was exhausted and near tears. Betsy helped me present my letters of recommendation—the Barbizon was terribly fussy and my certificate from Katharine Gibbs proved to be an immense asset—and when I was finally signed in and was alone at last in my tiny cabin of a room, I just gave over to tears. I stuffed the pillow in my mouth and sobbed and sobbed. I wept for Charlie Thurston and for my ruined life and for my late love Prentice Eton who now would never be my husband. I wanted Tice so badly. I wanted him to hold me and forgive me and tell me everything would be alright. I wept because I was exhausted and terribly, terribly frightened.

You couldn't have swung a cat, as my father used to say, in my room at the Barbizon. It had a window and a radiator and a single bed. It had a dresser, a little desk and a small armchair. But it also had privacy and it was all mine. I was away from the eyes and judgments of Boston and I was grateful.

I did get a typing job. Eventually. Only it wasn't the important war work I'd envisioned. Every morning at nine I reported to the typing pool at The New York Life Insurance Company. Rode up in an elevator and banged away on a Royal typewriter the size of a Buick. By afternoons, it was all I could do to keep my eyes open. I just wanted to sleep and sleep and sleep. It was the pregnancy, I suppose, but I could have curled up under my typing table and slept like one drugged.

Betsy Galbraith was kind and she helped keep my secret, but we both knew it was just a matter of time. I couldn't stay at the Barbizon once my condition became evident. The Barbizon had standards and morals so strict that by comparison, even my mother's looked lax.

I must say for Betsy, that she was very resourceful. Very

cosmopolitan too. She knew exactly where to turn—which was to the Florence Crittenden Home. And so, before I could be expelled from the Barbizon or fired from New York Life for reasons of moral turpitude, Betsy and I took a taxi down to East 12th Street and sat down in a sort of admitting office and began the process of my matriculation into the Florence Crittenden Home for Unwed Mothers.

There was a nationwide network of Florence Crittenden Homes that took in young women in these circumstances and housed them during the latter stages of their pregnancies, provided meals and gentle amusements, medical care and ultimately, delivery services in exchange for the unwed mother's baby. After delivery, the infant would be put up for adoption and the mother—rehabilitated by Florence Crittenden counseling—would return to her former life, hopefully reformed and able to secure a husband to whom she would bear legitimate children. The Home was a welcome port in a storm, for what else was I to do? I resigned myself to living for the next four months behind the red bricks of the respectable-looking building on East 12th Street that held its secrets well.

I was a model inmate. I got on well with several of the other young women, until, one by one, they graduated into the section of the Home set up for labor and delivery. In those days, a two-week post-delivery recuperation period of bed rest was mandated for maternal health, and when my friends had recuperated, they each walked out the double front doors onto the pavement of East 12th street never to be seen or heard from again.

I entered the Florence Crittenden Home in early July and so I spent the long, hot summer in Lower Manhattan visited only by Betsy Galbraith who made trips down by subway bringing me letters from home. My family was still writing to me at the Barbizon address and Betsy intercepted my mail and carried my letters back to East 63rd to be mailed and postmarked. Once in a while a thin, fragile V-mail envelope arrived from Tice, and I'd carry the letter to the bathroom where I could be sure of privacy, and there I would read it and weep with longing and shame. I was homesick, lovesick, morningsick and terribly scared that summer. And I was hot too, for it was sweltering in Manhattan and there was no air conditioning, just a fetid breeze that occasionally strayed up from the Battery.

October tenth was my due date. I woke that morning in breathless anticipation, certain that the birth was near, but it took another four days for things to get going. But finally I too made it to the labor room to begin the ordeal and deliverance.

Miss Robinson was my nurse. Elizabeth Robinson. She was younger than the other nurses and she had kind eyes. I remember that. I remember how her eyes looked above her mask—golden brown and kind. I remember her mask and then I was wearing a mask too. Miss Robinson gently placed the anesthetic mask over my mouth and nose and then it was all over.

I opened my eyes slowly and Miss Robinson was there.

"Girl or boy?" I said. I was terribly groggy.

"You had a beautiful little girl," she said. "She is healthy."

"May I hold her?" I said.

And Miss Robinson shook her head.

"You know the rules, Arabella. You signed the paper. You know that it is against Florence Crittenden policy to show the baby to the mother."

Oh yes, policy. I knew about that. New mothers were not to see their babies. They were not to hold them. They were not to name them. It was felt that the mothers would bond with their babies if they saw them, held them or named them, and then it would be more difficult to give them up for adoption. I knew that. It had been explained to me when I'd come to Florence Crittenden. It had even made sense to me. Then. And I'd signed the contract willingly. But now—now that my baby had been born—my daughter—didn't I deserve to at least look at her?

"But can't I just see her? Just see her for a minute?" I begged.

And Miss Robinson's eyes were troubled and for a minute I thought she was going to break the rule for me. But then she shook her head and her eyes were sad.

"I'm so sorry Arabella, but I can't do that. I can't go against policy."

And she turned away.

It seems to me that I shed more tears that year than I had in all the years of my life added together. And as I was wheeled away to the room where I'd complete my recovery, I quietly shed some more.

Well, they could keep me from seeing my daughter and from holding her, but they couldn't prevent me from naming her! And so privately, silently, I named her Jill. I had never known a Jill, so she wasn't named after anyone. But with a name of her own, she became a person. A distinct individual. And I tried to imagine what she'd look like. Would she look like Charlie Thurston? Would she look like me? I prayed that the woman whom Jill would come to know as 'mother' would be kind and wise. That she would be a woman who desperately wanted a daughter and who would accept this precious gift with the deepest gratitude and the greatest care.

I lay there in the hospital bed and followed Jill all through her infancy and her childhood, all through her grade school years. I imagined how she'd look at school dances in her first long gown and at football games in a camel's hair coat. I imagined her in a white gown on her wedding day. And in my imagination, I bonded with the image of my daughter. Florence Crittenden couldn't prevent that.

After two weeks, I was pronounced recovered from childbirth and rehabilitated from my wanton ways. So with my suitcase, I too, stepped out onto the pavement of East 12th Street.

I couldn't return to the Barbizon and I no longer had a job at New York Life, so the only option was to go home. I took the subway up to Penn Station and accomplished my trip to Boston in reverse order from my arrival. The station and the train cars were still as crowded, but I no longer felt any nausea. I just felt exhausted. Depleted and empty like a little balloon that has lost most of its air and so is soft with a few wrinkles like skim on a cup of cocoa. And I looked out the train window and didn't see a blessed thing except Jill.

But one good thing came out of that train ride home. I decided as we swayed along, that there should be other avenues open to young women—ways for them to avoid unwanted pregnancies. I made up my mind to do what I could to serve that goal. I'd heard of the Planned Parenthood League and I knew that it was illegal in Massachusetts. I didn't care. Illegal or not, I decided to pledge my time and money to the cause of preventing unwanted pregnancies. I made fists of my two hands that were folded in my lap and I made a silent pledge. I'm pleased to say it is a pledge I've been able to keep.

My family seemed glad to have me home. The British evacuees were still in residence, and Olivia and Julian had grown and become Americanized and therefore noisier. But they were a welcome distraction. Olivia had taken over my room and so I moved in with her and had a little roommate for a while. It was Indian summer in Boston and I took long walks around the Common and the Public Garden. Sat on a bench and watched the crew put away the swan boats for the coming winter. Scuffled my feet through the fallen leaves. The scent of burning leaves was in the air. Then the weather turned colder and before the ice rink froze on the Common, we got word that Tice was coming home.

I was nervous. Would he be different? Would he notice changes in me?

He came directly to Pinckney Street from the station and suddenly there he was in the drawing room. He set his duffle bag down and held his arms out wide. And then I was against his chest and it was all right again. Everything was all right. He was thinner, limping from his leg wound, but he was home.

"How soon can we be married?" he said.

Well, Prentice's father was quite ill and we had to make some compromises in our plans, but we did get married as soon as we possibly could. We had a little service in the drawing room at Pinckney Street with my sister Martha as my only attendant. There was still no white gown—and I wouldn't have felt right about wearing one. I wore a simple dress—blue—and we left for a weekend honeymoon in Montreal. Then Tice and I got right into the business of making a life together and to the business of forgetting about the lives we had lived during the war years. Tice didn't like to talk about the war; he just wanted to put it behind him. So he didn't ask me about my war years either. Which was fine with me.

Prentice was immersed immediately in the family business and, somewhat to my surprise, I found myself pregnant again. Tice was thrilled. He so badly wanted a son to carry on the Eton name, and while I wanted that for him—and while I didn't ever dare say it—I hoped for a daughter. And when Caroline was born, and when I was holding her at last, I thought of Jill. Then within another year and a half, Tice had his son. George. But George was the last child we were to have. I don't know why. No more babies arrived. Life was busy and life was good. But every year on October 14th, I thought of Jill. I still do. Every blessed year. My daughter. My only surviving daughter. She is somewhere and I pray she is well.

Chapter 47

Nell sat motionless as the emotion of writing Bella's story drained out of her. When you are a writer, she thought, you take into yourself the shadows and energies of your subject. You absorb emotions that weren't originally yours and sometimes those emotions can be dangerous. She remembered an energy worker she'd once seen—a massage therapist named Loretta something—who'd concluded her energy work with vigorous wiping motions all down her arms as if she were stripping off soiled clothing. Then she shook off this invisible 'soiled' energy the way a dog that has stepped in something unwanted, shakes a hind leg.

Nell rose slowly and moved toward the kitchen, prowling aimlessly. She turned an unfocused stare on the Aga, as if she couldn't imagine its purpose or what it was doing here in her kitchen.

It's true, she thought, wandering out of the kitchen toward the front of the house, you take on attributes of your characters, but on the other hand, aren't all characters simply incarnations of some part of the writer's psyche? In writing, the barrier between subject and writer becomes a permeable membrane—a vaporous curtain—and the writer travels back and forth between these planes and sometimes the journey can be dangerous. Reality becomes unfocused as the writer drifts in some kind of artistic limbo between these real and astral worlds.

She'd nailed it though, Bella's story. A slam-dunk. She had a solid conviction of that. She would give this draft a few days to rest. Give it a soaking period. She'd soak the draft the way she'd soak a casserole dish in the sink until it was ready to scour. Then she'd scrub the draft through revision and carry it to Salem. She imagined Bella's reaction. This "amendment" was a bold move—an act of bravery. Bella had been inspired by Brittany's clear-eyed fortitude. By Brit's determination to have her child openly and honestly. And thus inspired, Bella felt she could do no less. Nell was deeply moved.

"This introspection isn't healthy!"

Nell said this aloud. She shook her head as if to clear it and went to find the aspirin.

Chapter 48

Robert Hutchins and Jerry Gasso were coming to dinner, and Robert was bringing the first revised copy of *Looking Forward*. As she cluttered about the kitchen, Nell found she was excited to see it. In honor of the occasion, she was making pheasant and lentil soup, a dish that in Nell's opinion, sounded more exotic than it tasted, but once you got your hands on the pheasant, the rest of the preparation was duck soup. Or pheasant soup, in this case.

The new book wasn't the only reason Nell was looking forward to the evening. Nell wanted a current events report and she meant to prize it out of Robert.

"Nellybean!" Jerry Gasso cried as he pushed his way out of the car. "Gorgeous to see you! And, as usual, you're looking gorgeous."

"You're just hungry, Jerry," she told him. "and you want to butter me up."

"Ta-da," Robert said, holding out a copy of *Looking Forward*. "Signed, sealed and delivered, Ms. Bane."

"Has Bella seen it?"

"She has. And she claims to be well satisfied. Says this revision was the second-to-last thing on her bucket list and now it is accomplished."

"The second to last?" Nell was bewildered. "What is the last?"

"A trip to Boston to see John Dockery. Which we accomplished today, as a matter of fact. Bella wanted to look over her will. Wanted to make a few changes."

"Well!" said Nell, "I shouldn't wonder!" And her writer's mind began to make speculative leaps. "Am I to know a bit of what went on?"

Robert Hutchins smiled.

"In due time," he told her enigmatically. "I thought I would open some wine first."

Nell collected three wine glasses from the cupboard. She placed down a board with some cheese, a knife, a quartered pear, some crackers and a dish of olives. She looked pointedly at Robert Hutchins, but he appeared to be studying the color of the wine in his glass. Over the rim of his own glass, Jerry Gasso gave her an ironic smile and a wink. Nell had waited long enough.

"John Dockery," she mused, needling to have her curiosity satisfied. "He's Bella's attorney. Do you know him, Robert?"

Robert settled back in his chair. He was finally ready to tell his story.

"Most certainly. John's father was the Etons' lawyer for years until he retired and his son took over the practice. John and his father were my parents' attorneys as well. John's a good man. He has set up a number of trusts for the Etons—charitables, family trusts, that sort of thing. I was executor of Tice's will so I've seen quite a bit of John in the last month or so, and I am Bella's executor as well. That's why I had to be in on the changes she needed to make."

"Needed to make," Nell repeated.

"That's right. First Bella wanted to make certain that Frank and Henny would be in comfortable positions after she dies. She has made generous bequests to both. She also wanted to review the charitable trusts and she made a few minor changes there."

Robert paused thoughtfully. He steepled his fingers and tapped them on his chin, apparently considering. Nell was accustomed to Robert's contemplative narrations but this present interlude made her want to scream. She thought of lunging at him and shaking out of him the information she wanted. The short parade of Eton heirs marched into her mind led by the Grands, colorless bit players; extras who quickly left the stage to be followed by the Greats—the lovely and enigmatic Brittany, crass Indigo of the bulging grape-green eyes and blue hair, and finally Derek. Sullen. Sneering. In her mind's eye Nell saw Bella's fingers curling toward the crystal vase and heard her hurl words at her great-grandson that she'd never spoken in her life. And she heard Derek's derisive laughter as turned his back on his great-grandmother and sauntered insultingly from the room.

"Robert. I have to know. Did she cut Derek out of her will?"

Robert smiled.

"She did not. Oh, she trimmed his inheritance a bit and pushed it out a bit—that is, made his inheriting date later—but her reasoning went along these lines. Derek is family. He may be pond scum, but it is the Eton pond. She is disappointed in him. Very disappointed. You might even say heartsick. But she has worked very hard to forgive him for what he did to Tice. And she acknowledges that over the generations there have been a few bad apples hanging on the Eton and Whiteside family trees, but given time, the good stock—the stronger stock—has always dominated. Won out. Derek Eton might sire a child who will turn out to redeem the father's weaknesses. Or perhaps that task will be left to one of Derek's grandchildren. Or even to a great-great-grandchild. Bella knows she will never see this happen, but she trusts that it will happen. And she is willing to take a chance on him. This, after all, is family. You have to accept them. You have to believe in them. And finally, you have to love them."

Nell sat quietly, letting these facts sink in. She sighed.

"There is a base and vile part of me, Robert, that would like to see Derek Eton punished—cast out—for his callous treatment of Tice, for his complete disregard for his great-grandfather's welfare, for his rude treatment of Bella, and for his lack of human...well, human decency. It is hard to have to admit these feelings, especially in the face of Bella's generosity and decency. I am ashamed."

"Well, move over, Nellybean," Jerry Gasso said. "You have plenty of company on that little island of shame. You'll have to share it with Henny and Frank. They're not about to forgive and forget. And if you're taking a census, you'd better include me."

A little silence settled over the trio. Then Nell sighed again.

"Time for sustenance," she said. "Time for some pheasant and lentil soup."

PHEASANT AND LENTIL SOUP
1 small pheasant cleaned
7-1/2 cups water
1 onion thickly sliced
1 large carrot thickly sliced
2 stalks of celery chopped
1 bay leaf 8 peppercorns
Fresh sprig of thyme

2/3 cup brown lentils
2 small leeks trimmed and chopped
salt and pepper to taste.

Put the pheasant in a large stockpot, cover with water, bring to a slow boil and skim the surface. Add the remaining ingredients except the lentils and leeks. Cover and simmer 45 minutes. Remove the pheasant; when it is cool enough to handle, remove the breast meat and return the carcass to the soup pot and simmer for 2 more hours. Strain the stock through a sieve that is set over a bowl. Cool and refrigerate the stock, the reserved breast meat and the best bits of the leg meat. Refrigerate overnight. The next day, remove the layer of fat on the surface, return the pan to the stove and bring stock to a boil—reduce stock to 6 cups by simmering, adding water if necessary.

Add the lentils and leeks to the stock, cover and simmer 45 minutes until the lentils are tender. Meanwhile, dice the reserved meat and add it to the soup. Season with salt and pepper and simmer a few more minutes till heated through.

Chapter 49

Arabella Eton and Henny DeFelice had the front door open and were standing there even before Nell put a foot on the first granite step. Nell was slightly surprised by how pleased she was to see them and there were hugs from both.

"Well, you two look excited," Nell said. "And you look like you have another surprise up your sleeve, Bella. I'm beginning to think of you as the woman of mystery."

Bella tapped the side of her nose with her forefinger.

"A veritable Hawkshaw," she said. "Oh dear, that dates me terribly, doesn't it? Do either of you remember that cartoon from the 'twenties? No? Well, no matter! I've earned every one of my venerable years. Come in, dear. We're having tea in the kitchen and I've received a letter I can't wait to share."

"I've already read it," Henny bragged.

"And you're not going to hint at what it is?" Nell asked her.

Henny made a zipping motion across her mouth.

"My lips are sealed."

Bella poured three cups of tea. Then with great ceremony, she produced a letter in a sliced envelope and handed it to Nell. Nell examined the return address. Chicago. She slid out the sheets of letter paper.

Dearest Grandmother Bella, The first reason I'm writing is to tell you how very moved I was and how impressed I am with your amended story. You spoke of all the tears you shed during those terrible war years, and reading, I shed tears of my own. I treasure the copy of *Looking Forward* that you and Prentice gave me in Salem, and I cherish especially the beautiful inscriptions that you each wrote on the flyleaf. This second edition doesn't in any way diminish the value of the first. Nor does it replace it. Rather, it enlarges the story. Enriches it. Gives the first book another dimension and makes it so very personal.

There is one story, wrote the poet Robert Graves, *and one story only, that will prove worth your telling.*

And you have told it. At last. May it give you peace.

Now I have something to tell you. My baby has been born. She is a beautiful and healthy six-pound, five-ounce infant who is nineteen inches long. She sleeps and eats and wakes and cries and poops and does all the things a newborn is supposed to do. But she is awake quite a bit too, and when she's awake, she looks all around at this world that is new to her, and when she looks up at me, her face is full of wonder. I look back at her in the same way. I can hardly believe she is here and that she is mine. And she looks as if she can't quite figure out who I am but somehow knows that we will be together forever. I am delighted with her. And when I hold her, I think of you and the baby you weren't allowed to hold. What a marvelous, wondrous thing it is to hold your very own daughter. In the spring, we will come to Salem so you can hold her too—your first great-great-grandchild. I can't wait to introduce you. And now here is one thing more I have to tell you: I have named her Arabella. Arabella Jill.

Your loving Great-Granddaughter Brittany

Nell handed the letter back to Bella and tears were shining in her eyes. She wiped them away.

"What does that mean," asked Henny, "that part about there being only one story?"

"Well, there's been a lot of speculation about that," Nell said. "I think it can mean whatever you want to read into it, Henny. But there's general agreement that the poet was writing about myth, which is to say he was writing about the universal human experience of life that is, after all, the ultimate story. Others have pointed out that we want to hear people's stories but we also want to tell our own story."

"I think," Bella said slowly, "it means you have only one life and what you do with it is up to you. So the story you choose to tell has to be true. Honest. A lie isn't worthy of telling, is it? When I finally found the courage to tell my story the true way, it felt exactly right. It was the only story worth telling."

Arabella leaned forward and placed her hand over Nell's. "So you see, my dear," the old woman said, "it all happened just as Tice and I hoped it would. Well, not quite the way we expected, but in the end our wish is fulfilled. Family continues. It is perpetuated and at the same time, the antecedents are respected and revered."

"On the day I met you," Nell smiled, remembering, "Tice said there were Arabellas on your family tree going back four generations. Now there is an Arabella going forward. The name skipped three generations but here it is again. Looking forward—that's what you and Tice have lived for."

"I have a great-great-granddaughter," Bella said wonderingly. "Her name is Arabella Jill."

THE GHOST TIES A DOUBLE KNOT